Giada De Laurentiis's
Recipe for Adventure
Hawaii!

written with Brandi Dougherty
illustrated by Francesca Gambatesa

Grosset & Dunlap
An Imprint of Penguin Group (USA) LLC

This is dedicated to my nephew Julian, and to all the adventures that he
and Jade will encounter together, just like Alfie and Emilia!

GROSSET & DUNLAP
Published by the Penguin Group
Penguin Group (USA) LLC, 375 Hudson Street, New York, New York 10014, USA

USA | Canada | UK | Ireland | Australia | New Zealand | India | South Africa | China

penguin.com
A Penguin Random House Company

Library of Congress Cataloging-in-Publication Data is available.

ISBN 978-0-448-48391-7 (pbk)   10 9 8 7 6 5 4 3 2 1
ISBN 978-0-448-48392-4 (hc)   10 9 8 7 6 5 4 3 2 1

Chapter 1

Alfie and Emilia stood in the middle of the kitchen. Emilia had her hands on her hips, and Alfie had his arms crossed over his chest. They scowled at each other. The overflowing trash can sat on the floor between them.

"It's your turn!" Emilia cried.

Alfie shook his head. "No, it's not!"

They stared each other down.

"Well, I'm not doing it," Emilia finally said.

"Neither am I," Alfie replied.

"Alfredo!" Emilia shouted, using Alfie's full name.

Dad appeared in the doorway. *"Quietare!"* he said in Italian. "Quiet down. What's all the shouting about?"

"It's Alfie's turn to take out the garbage, and he won't do it," Emilia said.

"I did it last week!" Alfie cried.

"No, you didn't!" Emilia stomped her foot.

"Enough!" Dad held up his hands between them. "What's gotten into you two lately? You can't seem to get along for more than ten minutes at a time."

Alfie and Emilia were silent as they stared at the floor.

"Alfie, pick up the bag. Emilia, go open the garbage can in the garage. You can do it together," Dad said.

Alfie was about to protest again when he saw the serious look on Dad's face. Dad was not messing around. Alfie sighed, picked up the bag, and followed Emilia into the garage.

"I know it was your turn," Emilia whispered as she lifted the lid on the bin. "You're just being a *baby*."

Alfie rolled his eyes. Emilia could be such a know-it-all, especially now that she'd turned thirteen. She was only a year and a few months older than Alfie, but she liked to remind him of that fact every chance she got.

Alfie and Emilia stomped back through the kitchen and stood in the doorway to the family room. Dad had his back to them and was talking to their great-aunt Donatella.

"Maybe this is a bad weekend for us to go on our trip," Dad was saying. "Those two just can't seem to get along lately."

"*Nonsenso!* Nonsense!" Zia Donatella replied, sweeping aside her long salt-and-pepper hair. "You and Arianna have waited ages to have a weekend away. You deserve it."

"We have been looking forward to it . . . ," Dad said.

"We'll be fine here," Zia continued. "Don't you worry about a thing."

"All right, we'll stick to our plan." Dad picked up his briefcase. "Well, I'd better get to work. See you tonight."

"*Arrivederci!*" Zia called before turning to see Alfie and Emilia sulking in the doorway.

"Do you think we can all get along this weekend?" Zia asked. Alfie and Emilia nodded. "Good. Now, anything you want to do while your parents are away?"

"I want to play video games and maybe watch a movie!" Alfie said. "And we're going to cook, right?"

"Of course!" Zia said. Zia was an incredible cook, and ever since she'd come to stay with the Bertolizzi family, she'd taught Alfie and Emilia some amazing recipes she'd learned from her travels around the world.

Emilia made her way over to the sofa and flopped down. "*I* have a history presentation I need to get started on," she said, giving Alfie a look like she was being more responsible than he was.

"That should be fun." Zia perched on the arm of the sofa next to Emilia. Everybody knew that Emilia *loved* history. It was her favorite subject. Alfie, on the other hand, could never get enough of geography. His bedroom walls were plastered with maps of all kinds. And he was forever looking at maps online—everything from world maps to city maps—even climate maps!

"My presentation has to be on the history of a specific city or state," Emilia continued. "I just can't decide which to focus on!"

"Well, you've got plenty of options," Alfie replied, smiling at Zia. He thought about all the places they'd visited and experiences they'd had thanks to Zia's magical recipes. "You could talk about any of the cities we've gone to."

"I know," Emilia replied. "I just can't decide if I should present somewhere we've already been or somewhere new we might go!"

Zia nodded. "That's a tough decision."

"Not to me!" Alfie said. "I'd definitely give a talk about somewhere we've been. That's much easier. You could talk about the Christ the Redeemer statue in Rio de Janeiro, or the Eiffel Tower in Paris!"

Just then Mom walked down the stairs. "Who's going to the Eiffel Tower?" she asked.

Alfie looked at Zia, who busied herself picking lint off the arm of the sofa. Mom and Dad didn't know about any of Alfie and Emilia's adventures. It was their and Zia's little secret.

"Uh, no one," Emilia replied. "We were just talking about my history presentation."

"Oh, I just love Paris!" Mom gushed. "Eating fresh croissants every morning and going to all those sidewalk cafés . . ."

"And the markets!" Alfie chimed in; then his eyes widened as he realized what he'd said. "I mean, you know . . . I remember how Zia was telling us about the markets . . ."

Mom nodded, but looked a little confused.

"Well," Zia said, straightening the brightly colored stone necklace she always wore, "aren't you two going to be late for school?"

Mom glanced at the clock on the mantel. "Oh, goodness! It *is* late. Grab your stuff, kids. We've gotta go!"

"Bye, Zia!" Emilia said, giving her a quick hug.

"Bye!" Alfie gave Zia a grateful smile before slinging his backpack over his shoulder.

Zia winked. "Have a good day, *bambini!*"

Chapter 2

The next morning, Alfie rubbed his eyes as he shuffled into the kitchen, ready for breakfast. Every Saturday morning, Zia, Mom, and Dad made breakfast together. What they made was always a surprise, and it was always delicious—whether it was lemon-ricotta pancakes or breakfast burritos. But the kitchen was empty. Only silence filled the air—not a single mouthwatering food smell.

"Mom? Dad? Zia?" Alfie called, confused. Nobody answered.

Emilia burst through the kitchen door. "Where is everyone?" she asked. "What's for breakfast?"

"I don't know," Alfie said. "I'm going to check the garage."

"I'll go," Emilia said, jostling toward the door.

"No, I got it!" Alfie said, elbowing past Emilia.

Alfie and Emilia pushed through the door at the same time and spilled into the garage. The garage door was open, and Dad and Zia were standing in the driveway packing the car. Mom hustled past them with another bag.

"I'm ready!" she sang.

"You're leaving already?" Alfie asked, stepping lightly across the concrete in his bare feet.

"We want to get an early start, champ," said Dad. "It's a bit of a drive to the cabin."

"But we haven't had breakfast together yet!" Emilia said.

"Don't worry," Zia said. "We'll make breakfast as soon as they get on the road."

Alfie looked at Mom and Dad. Dad whistled as he

packed the car. Mom couldn't stop smiling. "Well, have a good time, I guess," Alfie said.

Mom swooped in and kissed Alfie's forehead. "We will! And you two be good for Zia. I don't want to hear about any more bickering, either, understood?"

"Yes, Mom," Alfie and Emilia said together.

Dad opened his wallet and pulled out what Alfie thought were several twenty-dollar bills. "Here's a little something extra for the weekend," he told them. "In case you guys want to take Zia out for a treat or something." Then he handed the cash to Alfie.

Alfie grinned and put the money in the pocket of his pajama pants. "Thanks, Dad!"

Emilia glared at Alfie for pocketing the money, but then managed a smile. "Yeah, thanks, Dad."

"Be good," Dad said, looking them both in the eyes.

"We will," they responded together.

Zia put her arms around Alfie's and Emilia's shoulders as they watched the car back down the driveway.

Dad honked the horn, and Mom waved before they pulled away.

"Now, let's go see about that breakfast, shall we?" Zia asked.

Back in the kitchen, Zia whipped up omelets with cheddar cheese and mushrooms while Emilia cut up some fresh fruit, and Alfie set the table. Breakfast was quieter than usual with Mom and Dad gone. They ate their food mostly in silence. Then Alfie flicked a piece of cantaloupe onto Emilia's plate just to annoy her. It worked.

"Alfie, *don't*!" Emilia said, breaking the silence.

"What?" he replied with a sly smile.

Zia stood up and sighed. "I think I'll take care of the kitchen cleanup myself. Why don't the two of you spend some time on your own this morning? Away from each other. Emilia, you can get started on your history report,

and Alfie, you can practice your drums."

"Okay, Zia," Emilia said.

Alfie took his plate to the sink and then headed out to the garage to his drum set. The spring band concert had been two weeks ago, and Alfie's drum solo had been a smashing success. Everybody told him how well he performed, and he knew his family was proud. Since the concert was over, Alfie didn't really have anything he needed to work on, but he always enjoyed playing. With all his practice—especially thanks to performing at Carnival in Rio—he was getting better and better. Alfie smiled, thinking of all the new friends he'd made thanks to Zia's adventures. He couldn't help but wonder when the next adventure might be.

Chapter 3

Later that afternoon, Zia called Alfie and Emilia into the kitchen. "I thought we'd make a snack," she told them.

"Good!" Alfie said. "I'm hungry."

Zia turned the oven on and starting pulling ingredients from the cupboards.

"What are we making?" Emilia asked, tying her golden-brown hair into a ponytail.

"We've got a bunch of very ripe bananas, so I thought we'd make banana bread before they go bad," Zia replied.

"Yum!" Alfie said. "I haven't had banana bread in ages. I think last time we had it, it was a loaf Mom picked up from the bakery counter at the grocery store."

Zia grimaced.

"That was before you came to stay, Zia," Alfie said.

"But now we make almost everything fresh from scratch!" Emilia added.

"And we have fun," Zia said, smiling.

Alfie thought so, too.

"Well, you're going to love this recipe," Zia continued. "It has chocolate chips and macadamia nuts in it." She placed flour, salt, baking powder, and baking soda on the counter. "Emilia, why don't you whisk these dry ingredients together in a bowl? Alfie, you can peel and mash the bananas. We need a cup and a half of banana for our mixture."

"I hope Mom and Dad have a good time this weekend," Emilia said as she measured and whisked.

Zia laughed. "I'm sure they will." She used a knife to chop the macadamia nuts into small pieces. "Alfie, are those bananas ready?"

"Yes!" Alfie said, holding up his measuring cup.

"*Eccellente.* Let's put that in this bowl," Zia told him. "We need to mix in some vanilla and a little bit of Greek yogurt."

"Do you ever travel with friends on your adventures, Zia?" Emilia asked.

Zia wiped a smudge of flour from the end of Emilia's nose and smiled. "*Certamente.* Certainly. I've traveled with friends on lots of different trips."

"What was your favorite trip with friends?" Emilia asked.

"When I lived in Hawaii, my friends and I traveled between the islands all the time," Zia replied.

"You lived in Hawaii?" Alfie cried.

Zia nodded. "On Maui."

"I didn't know that. How cool."

"As a matter of fact," Zia said, "that's where this banana bread recipe is from. I learned to make it while I was there. I had a friend in Maui who introduced me to a fabulous Hawaiian woman, and she taught it to me.

She had a famous roadside stand where she sold her
banana bread, and people would travel from all over the
island to buy it. My recipe has evolved over the years,
but that's where it came from originally. And it was my
amico's, my friend's, favorite."

Emilia and Alfie had both stopped stirring as they
listened to Zia.

Zia took another large bowl and a hand mixer from the cupboard. "Emilia, can you add the sugar, brown sugar, and butter to this bowl? We'll mix those together until they're light and fluffy."

Emilia dumped her ingredients into the bowl and turned on the mixer. After a few minutes, Zia cracked an egg and added that to Emilia's mix. Then she added Alfie's bananas mixed with vanilla and yogurt. *"Perfetto!"* Zia said. "Now it's time to fold in the dry ingredients."

Alfie grabbed the other bowl and tilted it toward Emilia's bowl, letting the flour mixture slide into the wet batter.

"Slow down!" Emilia said as she stirred the mixture with a spatula.

"You should stir faster," Alfie replied.

"Okay, okay," Zia said. "You're both doing fine."

Emilia continued folding slowly until the mixture was combined. Then Zia sprinkled in the chopped macadamia nuts and mini chocolate chips.

Alfie grabbed a nut from the cutting board. "I've never had macadamia nuts before," he said, biting into the light yellow nut. He liked the crunch and the sweetness of it.

"Macadamia nuts are a staple in Hawaii," Zia said. "And they're perfect for making sweet treats like banana bread and brownies."

"Yum!" Emilia exclaimed.

Once all the ingredients were combined, Zia picked up a loaf pan and coated the sides with butter. She dusted flour over the buttered pan, then used a spatula to ease the batter in. Once it was scraped into the loaf pan, she popped it into the oven. "The bread has to bake for almost an hour," she said. "Alfie, why don't you go grab a deck of cards? We'll play rummy while we wait."

Alfie dashed to the family room and took a deck of cards from the drawer in the coffee table. Back in the kitchen, Zia and Emilia had just finished putting the ingredients away. They settled onto stools around the island while Alfie shuffled the cards.

"What's Maui like?" Emilia asked.

"Breathtaking!" Zia sighed.

"I was just reading about Hawaii in my geography book," Alfie said. "It's the most remote chain of islands in the entire world!"

"Whoa," said Emilia.

"It definitely doesn't feel like you're in the United States when you're there, that's for sure," Zia added.

"Is it like Rio?" Alfie asked as he dealt the cards. He could picture the beaches of Rio de Janeiro jutting out on one side of the street and high rises on the other, with green rain forest and tall mountains all around.

"A little bit." Zia nodded. "There are obviously lots of beaches and that same lush vegetation that you see in Rio. And there are mountains and valleys on Maui just like in Rio—only the mountains are actually volcanoes."

"Wow!" Emilia exclaimed.

"Very wow," Zia agreed.

Alfie drew a card from the deck and arranged his hand

before discarding another card.

"Another big difference between Rio and Maui is that there are *a lot* fewer people on Maui," Zia continued. "It has much more of a laid-back island vibe."

"I like laid-back," Emilia said. "Rio was pretty intense!"

Zia laughed as she placed a set of hearts on the table. "You won't find that intensity in Maui. It's much more about taking things slow and enjoying little moments. And you'll never meet nicer people in your life. Everyone is friendly and treats you like family. It's that *aloha* spirit."

"I thought *aloha* meant hello," Alfie said.

"No, it means good-bye," Emilia argued.

"No, it doesn't!" Alfie shot back.

Zia held up her hands between them. "It means both hello and good-bye. But it's so much more than that. It's almost like a way of life—to live with respect for yourself and for others."

"That's cool," Alfie said. "It sounds nice."

"Totally," Emilia agreed.

Once they'd finished a couple of rounds of rummy, Zia hopped off her stool to check on the banana bread. "Almost done," she said.

Alfie breathed in the warm, sweet smell of the rich bread as it wafted through the air. "I can't wait."

"I actually don't know much about the history of Hawaii," Emilia said.

"Really?" Alfie said in surprise. His sister seemed to know something about every place!

Emilia gave her brother a look.

"It's an interesting history," Zia said. "It's a blend of a lot of different cultures."

"Is the food that way, too?" Alfie asked.

"Definitely!" Zia said. "Hawaiian food is influenced by places as different as Portugal, China, the Philippines, and Japan. But of course every dish has a distinct island flavor that you can't find anywhere else."

Just then the kitchen timer went off. Zia jumped up

again and opened the oven. She stuck a toothpick into the middle of the bread and pulled it out. "It's done!"

Alfie and Emilia both hopped up to look at the bread. It was a dark golden brown on top. "We'll let it cool for a few," Zia said.

Alfie reluctantly took his seat at the kitchen island again. "I don't know if I can wait that long!"

They played another round of rummy until the bread was cool. Alfie put the cards away as Zia cut the bread into thick slabs and placed a slice each on three small plates. Alfie picked up his whole slice of bread and brought it to his nose. It was dense and heavy, and the inside of the bread was a lighter color than the crust. It was pale yellow with dark black flecks of banana and bits of nuts and chocolate throughout. And it smelled delicious.

"I used to make this banana bread almost every week

on Maui," Zia said. "We'd pack up a few slices and some fresh tropical fruit and head down to the beach. We'd spend the whole day on the soft white sand. Sometimes we'd snorkel or surf or paddleboard. Other times we'd just watch the whales in the water."

"That sounds amazing, Zia," Alfie said. He watched Emilia break off a small bite of banana bread from her slice and bring it to her mouth. Alfie quickly did the same, closing his eyes as he bit through the slightly crispy crust to the moist banana-and-nutty richness inside. Alfie was about to ask Zia if she'd really gone surfing when all of a sudden his stomach dropped, like when an elevator goes down just a little too quickly . . .

Chapter 4

Alfie opened his eyes and squinted against the bright sun. He checked quickly to make sure Emilia was by his side. She shaded her eyes as they took in their surroundings. Alfie could see tall palm trees lining a pathway that led toward a body of deep blue water in the distance. The palms swayed gently in the breeze, waving their fronds toward the inviting water.

"Is that the ocean?" Emilia asked.

"It looks like an ocean," Alfie said. "Look at those waves."

"Do you think we're in Maui?" she asked.

"Aloha," Alfie heard behind him. He and Emilia swung

around to see two women wearing grass skirts and wreaths of flowers circling their heads like crowns. They stood in front of a tan building that rose up against the blue sky, which was dotted with puffy white clouds.

"We must be," Alfie whispered to Emilia.

One of the women stepped forward and placed a lei around Emilia's neck. Then she placed another one around Alfie's neck. The light scent of the fresh flowers was sweet, like honey. Alfie gently touched one of the white petals. It felt like thick silk.

"Thank you," Emilia said, touching her own lei. "It's so beautiful!"

The woman smiled and nodded. She stepped back a pace as the other woman stepped forward. She extended the tray that balanced on her palm. There were two tall glasses with wedges of pineapple stuck to the rims. "Would you like some fresh pineapple juice?" she asked.

"Yes, please," Alfie said, reaching out eagerly.

"Thank you," Emilia said again as she took her glass.

Beads of water ran down the outside of the cool glass as Alfie took a drink from the straw. The juice was a bit thick and pulpy, and it had a perfect pineapple sweetness to it. Alfie could tell it was fresh and not from a can.

"This is delicious," Emilia said. Alfie nodded in agreement, too busy finishing off his juice to speak.

Alfie and Emilia put their empty glasses back on the tray.

"Thank you," Alfie finally said.

"You're welcome." The woman smiled. Then she gestured toward the open doors of the building behind her. "Welcome to the Grand Lahaina Maui Resort."

Alfie beamed and strode confidently up the path to the resort entrance. He stopped when he realized that Emilia was trailing behind him. "Come on!" he said.

Emilia still hesitated. She smiled at the women again and then hurried to Alfie's side. "They think we're staying here," she whispered.

"So?" Alfie said as they stepped through the doorway

and into the hotel lobby. It was a wide-open space with big potted plants and hanging baskets of flowers everywhere. Sunlight shone through an enormous skylight high above them. It looked like a greenhouse. He couldn't help but smile as he took it all in. This place was amazing.

"*So,* I don't want to get in trouble!" Emilia said through gritted teeth.

Alfie sighed. "We're not going to get in trouble," he told her.

"Look at this place, Alfie," Emilia continued. "It's super nice. There's no way we could afford it."

"Come on, Emilia," Alfie said. "Where's your sense of adventure?"

Emilia opened her mouth to argue again.

"Let's just look around, okay?" Alfie said.

"Fine," Emilia said, her eyes darting around the lobby nervously.

Alfie nudged Emilia forward. He really hoped she wasn't going to be a stick-in-the-mud the whole time. This was the start of a new adventure, after all. He wanted to make the most of it!

Chapter 5

Alfie led the way across the lobby and out a side door next to the registration desk. Down a few steps and off to the right was a huge pool sparkling in the sun. Deck chairs and umbrellas ringed the edge of the pool, and larger lounge chairs that almost looked like beds were set back from the pool near patches of thick grass. There were kids splashing in the water or floating on brightly colored foam noodles. "See," Alfie said to Emilia. "There are tons of kids here."

Alfie led Emilia down the palm tree–lined path, which wrapped around the side of the pool and then away toward the beach. At the edge of the beach there was a wooden cabana with a big RENTALS sign. It wasn't yet open for the day, but Alfie read the list of all the equipment you could rent: surfboards, boogie boards, stand-up paddleboards, and snorkel gear. Alfie thought he might burst from excitement. He wanted to try all of those things!

Resort workers were busy setting up more lounge chairs and umbrellas in rows facing the ocean. "This resort is fancy," Alfie said.

"That's what I was trying to tell you!" Emilia replied.

"We'll be fine." Alfie smiled. "We always are!"

Emilia nodded. Alfie knew she couldn't argue with that. Even though they never knew what to expect on their adventures, everything always worked out!

"Let's go check out the rest of the hotel," Alfie said. "We'll come back to the beach later."

They made their way back up the path and into the hotel lobby. They passed a cool-looking resort store and a big restaurant with white tablecloths and vases of flowers on each table, and then saw an open courtyard with a buffet in the middle. Resort workers were in the process of removing trays and dishes of food.

"Too bad," Alfie said, gesturing toward the buffet area.

They circled around the lobby once more and stopped in front of a bank of elevators.

"Want to go up to the top floor?" Alfie asked. "Maybe there's a roof deck and we can get a view of the area."

"Okay," Emilia said, hurrying into an open, empty elevator. She pushed the CLOSE button a few times. Alfie knew she didn't want anyone else to join them in the elevator and ask any questions.

They reached the top floor and stepped into the hallway. Alfie heard two women talking. He peeked around the corner and saw two housekeepers standing next to a cleaning cart, chatting.

"Ugh, that suite takes forever to clean!" one of them said.

"I know!" said the other. "Please tell me no one is scheduled to stay there this weekend."

"Let me check." The woman opened a binder and slid her finger down the page. "We're in luck," she said. "It's empty on the schedule until next Thursday."

"You just made my day!"

The two women laughed.

Alfie and Emilia peered around the corner again and watched as the women wheeled the cart farther down the hallway. Emilia spotted something on the floor. She bent down to pick it up. It was a plastic key card. Alfie saw her look toward the housekeepers and open her mouth to speak.

"Shhhh!" Alfie whispered. He grabbed the key card and slid it into the slot of the suite door. A little green light flashed on the door panel and then it opened! Alfie smiled and stepped inside. Emilia's eyes got wide. She glanced down the hallway and then followed Alfie into the room, closing the door quietly behind her.

Alfie sucked in a breath as he took in the suite. It looked more like an apartment than a hotel room! There was a huge bed facing a giant flat-screen TV that was mounted on the opposite wall. Beyond the TV was a doorway to a separate room with another enormous bed, as well as a desk and a sofa. The far wall of the suite was all windows. Alfie stepped into the bathroom to see a tub the size of a small swimming pool along with a separate shower that was bigger than his bedroom.

"Alfie, look!" Emilia called from the other room. Alfie stopped staring at the shower and went out to see what Emilia was looking at. She smiled as she slid open one of the giant windows. It was actually a sliding-glass door leading out to a private terrace. Alfie ran over and joined Emilia on the balcony. The warm ocean breeze hit his face as he looked out at the row of big resort buildings and to the gleaming ocean beyond.

"This is so cool!" he said.

"I know," Emilia said, sounding a little breathless.

"Well, I think we know where we're staying in Maui." Alfie beamed.

Emilia's smile faltered a little. "Do you really think we should?"

"You heard the housekeepers," Alfie said. "No one is going to be here all week. It's perfect!"

Alfie walked inside, kicked off his shoes, and fell backward onto the king-size bed.

"Okay . . . ," Emilia finally said. "As long as we keep it clean for the housekeepers."

"Agreed," Alfie said, closing his eyes.

"Now get off my bed," Emilia said, sliding off her shoes and giving Alfie's leg a shove. "I want to sleep in this room."

"No way!" Alfie jumped up and stood on top of the bed. "I claimed it first."

Emilia jumped onto the bed, too. "But I'm the oldest!"

"So?" Alfie shouted, jumping up and down.

"Shhhh!" Emilia hissed. "Do you want to get us kicked out before we've even gotten to stay?"

"I got here first," Alfie said in a much quieter voice.

Emilia hopped off the bed. "Fine. We'll take turns. You can have this room tonight, but then I get it tomorrow night."

"Fine," Alfie said as he continued to bounce.

"Fine," Emilia said again. She walked into the other room and flopped down on that bed, annoyed.

Alfie couldn't help but grin. He'd won the best room for the first night!

Chapter 6

After Alfie got tired of jumping, he collapsed onto his bed and looked into Emilia's room. He wasn't sure if they were still arguing or not.

"Wanna go back down to the beach?" Alfie asked tentatively.

"Sure," Emilia answered, a little quiet.

Alfie stood up and stretched. "I can't wait to get in the water!" he said, trying to lighten the mood. "If it's anything like the Copacabana beach in Rio, it's going to be awesome!"

Emilia smiled. "Yeah."

Alfie headed toward the suite door.

"Wait, we need to bring the key card!" Emilia said, picking it up from the table.

"Oh, right," Alfie replied. "Here, I'll put it in my pocket."

"Don't lose it." Emilia handed him the plastic card. "And what's the suite number? We can't forget that, either."

Alfie opened the door and looked at the outside. "It's 1201."

"Okay, that's easy," Emilia said.

Alfie slid the key card into his pocket and closed the door behind them while Emilia hit the elevator button. Alfie could see her getting nervous as they waited, but the doors opened and it was empty.

They rode down a few floors before Emilia said, "Wait!"

"What?" Alfie looked alarmed.

"We don't have bathing suits!"

Just then the elevator doors opened into the lobby,

and Alfie spotted the resort store. He grinned and pulled Emilia toward it. "Problem solved!" he said.

"With what money?" Emilia asked.

"Have you forgotten already?" Alfie asked his sister. He dug in his jeans pocket and held the twenties their dad had given them up to Emilia's face. "Like I said, problem solved."

Emilia grinned back and darted into the store. Alfie followed and went straight for a rack of board shorts.

Before long, Alfie had picked out a pair of blue Hawaiian-print board shorts and a T-shirt. Emilia found a bright yellow bathing suit and a light cotton dress. They also bought a tube of sunscreen and two pairs of flip-flops from the sale bin.

When the clerk rang up the total, Alfie gulped. He looked at Emilia, whose mouth had dropped open. Alfie handed the clerk all the money he had. He got two dollars and twenty-three cents in return. They shuffled out of the store.

"I thought we'd have plenty of money left over for other stuff," Alfie said, still in shock.

"Me too," Emilia replied.

They headed back up to their room to change into their suits and put on sunscreen. Emilia found two fluffy beach towels in the closet, and soon they were on their way down to the lobby again.

They walked outside, and Alfie took in the smell of the ocean breeze and saw the glistening waves folding onto the sand in the distance. "Let's go!" he cried as he ran down the path to the water, his flip-flops clapping on the cement.

Chapter 7

When Alfie reached the end of the path, and his feet hit the sand, he kicked off his flip-flops and buried his toes. The sand was white, superfine, and really soft. It felt so good—warm, but not hot. He closed his eyes and wiggled his toes.

"Aloha," said a voice.

Alfie opened his eyes to see an older teenager standing next to him. He was tall and wore board shorts and a long-sleeved shirt with a necklace of small white shells on a leather cord.

"Hi!" Alfie replied.

"Are you guys here for the surf lesson?" the boy asked.

Without even thinking, Alfie said, "Yes!" He could see Emilia shift uncomfortably next to him. Alfie wasn't sure how Emilia felt about surfing, but he wasn't about to pass up the chance to learn!

"Sweet!" The boy smiled wide. "My name's Kai. Welcome to the Grand Lahaina."

"Thanks. I'm Alfie, and this is my sister, Emilia."

"You look like you could be about the same ages as my younger brother and sister," Kai replied.

"I'm thirteen," Emilia piped up. "And Alfie's eleven."

Alfie glared at his sister. She loved to tell everyone that she was older. "But I'll be twelve in a couple of months," Alfie added.

Kai whistled and motioned to two kids who were leaning on the counter inside the rental cabana. They dashed across the sand.

"What's up, bro?" the boy asked Kai.

"Jacob and Lana, meet Alfie and Emilia. They're here for the surf lesson, and you guys are the same age."

"Cool," Jacob said. "You're thirteen, too?"

"Yeah," Emilia said, smiling wide. "Hi."

"Let's get you guys your boards and your rash guards," Jacob said, motioning them over to the rental cabana.

"What's a rash guard?" Alfie asked.

"It's a long-sleeved surf shirt, like the one Kai is

wearing," Lana explained. "Basically it's like another layer of sunblock, but it also keeps your arms from chafing against your board when you paddle out."

"Good to know," Alfie said. Excitement was rising in his chest like soda bubbles. He had always wanted to try surfing, and now he was actually going to do it!

Alfie and Emilia put on their rash guards while Lana and Jacob chose surfboards for them. They laid the boards flat on the sand next to each other.

Kai walked over and stood on Alfie's board. "Before we even get in the water, you need to work on jumping up from a flat position on your board to a standing surf position."

Alfie and Emilia nodded.

"It's kind of like yoga, if you've ever done that," Kai continued.

Emilia nodded and smiled, but Alfie shook his head. Zia Donatella and Emilia liked to do yoga in the family room on Sundays, and they were always trying to get

Alfie to join them, but he never did.

"So, start by lying flat on your stomach on the board," Kai said. "Then you basically want to do a push-up and work on bringing your left leg forward to plant it just behind the midpoint of the board."

Alfie watched Emilia do this with no problem. He could do the push-up, but getting his leg forward in one quick motion was another story. Now he was beginning to wish he had joined Emilia and Zia for yoga all those Sundays!

"You want to get to the point where, with practice, you'll be able to just pop up into the correct stance in one motion without having to think about swinging that leg forward. But it's good to try it this way first just to get the movement going," Kai coached.

Alfie nodded and tried again. Jacob and Lana stepped forward to give extra pointers and demonstrate their own pop-up stances. They were really good!

"Great!" Kai said, after they'd been working on

the pop-up for a while. Alfie was starting to feel more comfortable. "Now we'll move on to a quick lesson on the proper stance for when you've caught a wave and you're up on your board."

Kai stepped onto Alfie's board again to demonstrate. "You want a wide stance, but not too wide. Make sure you're in the middle of the board for balance, and always keep your knees bent. Then lean forward slightly, but not too much or you'll just fall face-first into the water."

Alfie paid close attention to Kai's movements and positioning. Emilia, on the other hand, was either looking down the beach or smiling at Jacob.

They practiced their pop-ups and board stances for a little while longer. Finally, Kai said they were ready to get in the water. Alfie was giddy as he picked up his board and headed toward the small waves in front of the resort. Emilia trailed behind, talking to Lana.

Alfie's toes hit the water, and he was pleasantly surprised. It was even warmer than it had been in Rio!

Kai showed them how to paddle out into the waves and lean back when a wave was coming to keep the board above the water. Once they were out in the waves, they turned their boards to face the shore and got into position. Kai treaded water behind their boards to help them take turns catching a wave.

"Remember, when you fall, always fall flat so you don't plunge down into the water," Kai told them. "That way you won't run into any coral or rocks."

"And you definitely want to avoid the coral," Jacob chimed in. "That stuff is sharp!"

"Okay, here comes a good wave," Kai said. "Ready, Alfie?"

"Ready!" Alfie called back. He faced the shore and felt Kai give his board a push into the wave.

"Okay, pop up!" Kai shouted.

Alfie used his arms to push off his board and jumped up into position. He stood on wobbly legs for a few seconds before tipping forward into the water. He remembered to fall flat toward the surface and felt the surfboard tug against the tether around his ankle. He jumped back on the board and paddled toward Kai. He watched as Kai pushed Emilia's board into a wave. Emilia jumped up no problem, just as she'd done on the beach. She kept her legs bent and rode farther toward the shore before falling backward from her board. She popped up and squinted the water from her eyes.

"Nice job, Emilia!" Kai called.

With Kai's help, Alfie and Emilia caught wave after wave, but it was Emilia who rode them the easiest. She popped up from her board with ease and got the hang of it right away. Alfie struggled a bit more, but he really liked it.

After a while Emilia said she was done, and she and Lana paddled back to shore. Alfie felt like he could surf for hours longer, but he knew their lesson probably wasn't an all-day thing. He caught a few more waves, and then Kai said it was time to paddle in.

"You're getting the hang of it, Alfie," Kai told him.

"Definitely!" Jacob agreed.

"Thanks," Alfie said. Surfing was so fun!

"Are you sure Emilia's never done this before?" Jacob asked. "She's a natural."

Alfie frowned a little. "I'm sure."

Back on the beach, Kai put the surfboards and rash guards away while Alfie and Emilia toweled off.

"We're heading up to the resort restaurant," Lana told them. "Our uncle is the chef. He's working on the menu for a special luau this weekend, so we're stopping by for some snacks."

"Wow," Emilia said. "How cool!"

"You should come with us," Jacob said, smiling at Emilia.

"For sure," Lana added.

"That would be great," Alfie said.

"You know," Kai jumped in, "Uncle Gene has so much to do for this luau, I bet he could use some extra help."

"We'd be happy to help," Emilia said. "We cook with our great-aunt all the time."

"I could probably even throw in a free surf lesson in exchange," Kai said. "Assuming that's okay with your parents, of course."

"Totally!" Alfie cried. "Our parents won't mind at all!"

"I'm not so sure I want to surf again," Emilia said. "But I'm still happy to help with the luau."

"Have you ever tried hula dancing?" Lana asked. "Because I'm performing at the luau. I could always give you a hula lesson instead . . ."

Alfie saw Emilia's face light up. Anything dance-related was right up her alley, especially after she'd gotten to dance in two parades during Rio's Carnival.

"Oh my gosh!" Emilia gushed. "I would absolutely,

positively *love* to learn hula dancing!"

"Okay," Lana said. "When Alfie has his surf lesson, we'll do that, instead."

"Let's head to the restaurant," Jacob said, leading the way up the path.

Now Emilia was smiling as big as Alfie was. Their Maui adventure was well under way!

Chapter 8

A little brown lizard skittered across the path as Alfie and Emilia followed their new friends Lana and Jacob to the resort restaurant. This time, they curved to the left around the pool and ended up in a parking lot behind the resort. Jacob opened a door and waved Alfie and Emilia into the restaurant kitchen.

Inside the kitchen, there were cooks and waiters and dishwashers and bussers rushing all around. Big stainless-steel appliances and countertops ringed the open space. Lana and Jacob wove their way through the hectic kitchen and found a man with thick gray hair leaning against one of the spotless counters in the corner.

He was busily scribbling on a piece of paper.

"Hi, Uncle Gene," Lana said, giving the man a quick hug.

"Lana! Jacob! I'm so glad you're here!" The man had cheerful dark eyes and a big warm smile, but he looked a bit frazzled.

"These are our new friends, Alfie and Emilia," Jacob said.

"Is this your first time in Maui?" Uncle Gene asked.

"It is," Alfie and Emilia answered.

"Well, welcome to the Grand Lahaina."

"Thank you," the siblings replied.

"How's the luau prep going, Uncle Gene?" Lana asked.

"It was going okay until I found out that the mayor of

Maui and his entire staff will be attending!" Uncle Gene said.

"Wow. Really?" Jacob said.

"Yes," Uncle Gene answered. "The mayor's office called to say if the luau goes well, they'll want to use the Grand Lahaina to host the governor of Hawaii and several other state governors at an exclusive luau next month. The entire resort is rushing to put extra-special plans in place."

"That would be so big for you, Uncle Gene!" Jacob said.

Uncle Gene nodded, wiping his brow. "Yes, it would. It's exciting, but it's a lot more work at the last minute. After all, the luau is tomorrow!"

Lana put her hand on her uncle's shoulder. "We can help. Alfie and Emilia can, too."

Uncle Gene smiled wide. "Really? That's wonderful! At this point we need as many extra hands as possible!"

"We're happy to pitch in, sir," Alfie said. "We have

some experience helping in restaurants." Alfie thought about working with their friends at their restaurants in Hong Kong and New Orleans.

"You're old pros, then!" the chef replied. "And, please, call me Uncle Gene." He shuffled some papers around and pulled one out from the bottom of the pile. "Well, let me start by showing you the menu for our luau. Have you been to a luau before?"

"No, this will be our first one," Emilia answered. "We're very excited."

"You're in for a treat!" Uncle Gene said. "Luaus are a staple of Hawaiian culture."

"They're like big parties," Jacob interjected. "We always have one when there's a wedding or birthday or some other important family event."

"And, of course, the resort hosts them throughout the year so that tourists can get a taste of one of our traditions," Uncle Gene added. "Only this one will be even more spectacular!"

"How exciting!" Emilia said.

"So, the luau menu always starts with a *kālua* pig," Uncle Gene continued, pointing to the menu page.

"What's that?" Alfie asked.

"We cook a whole pig in an *imu*, which is an underground outdoor oven."

"Whoa!" Alfie said.

Uncle Gene laughed. "The resort has one down by the beach, dug into the dirt and lined with wood and rocks."

"When it's done, *kālua* pig basically looks and tastes like really good shredded pork," Lana added.

"Yum!" Emilia said.

"What else is on the menu?" Alfie asked. He was starting to get hungry just thinking about it!

"We have ahi poke, which is diced raw tuna marinated with some Maui onion and soy sauce, chicken long rice, which is like a Hawaiian-style chicken soup, sweet potatoes, poi—"

"What's poi?" Emilia asked.

"You're in luck," Uncle Gene said. "I just made some." He slid a ceramic bowl down the countertop toward Alfie and Emilia.

"It looks like purple pudding," Alfie said.

Uncle Gene, Jacob, and Lana laughed. "It definitely doesn't taste like pudding," Lana said.

Uncle Gene handed Alfie and Emilia each a small spoon. "Poi is made from boiled, mashed taro root. The taro root is a nice shade of purple."

Alfie lifted the spoon to his mouth. The consistency of the poi was like paste, and it kind of tasted that way, too—like glue you might use for an art project at school. He tried not to make a face as he set the spoon back on the counter. He definitely wouldn't be going for seconds.

Emilia had a similar look on her face. Her nose was wrinkled, and she tried to smile as she swallowed the starchy substance.

Jacob and Lana laughed again. "I think poi is an acquired taste," Jacob said, grabbing a spoonful.

"It's not my favorite," Lana added. "And I'm Hawaiian!"

Uncle Gene held back a laugh. "Let's move on to the desserts, shall we?"

Alfie and Emilia nodded furiously.

"We'll be serving lots of fresh tropical fruit grown here on the island as well as *malasadas, haupia,* and pineapple upside-down cake."

"I haven't heard of those first two things," Alfie said. "But I've never had a dessert I didn't like!"

Uncle Gene chuckled. "I have some *haupia* left over from this morning's breakfast buffet," he said, walking to the refrigerator and returning with a plastic container. It was full of small white cubes that looked like perfectly square, smooth marshmallows. He handed a piece to each of them.

"I love your *haupia,* Uncle Gene," Lana said, taking a bite.

Alfie took a bite, too. It tasted like sweet coconut custard.

"That's really good," Emilia said.

Just then a man in a white chef's jacket hurried over to Uncle Gene with an angry look on his face.

"I don't know how you expect me to get all this work done before the luau!" the man said, waving a list in front of Uncle Gene. His face was red and pinched.

"Pika, you remember my niece and nephew Lana and Jacob," Uncle Gene said with a measured tone. "And these are their new friends, Alfie and Emilia. This is my sous-chef, Pika. He's my second in command."

"Hi," Pika mumbled.

"We all have a lot to do—especially now with the

mayor coming," Uncle Gene continued. "We're splitting up the responsibilities as best we can. Everybody needs to pitch in and do a little extra."

"There's just no way I can get this all done in time," Pika argued.

"You're the sous-chef," Uncle Gene said, his voice rising a bit. "If you don't want the responsibility, I will find someone who does!"

Pika opened his mouth to argue again, but then looked around at Alfie and the others. "Fine," he grumbled before storming out of the kitchen and into the dining room.

Uncle Gene sighed and shook his head. "Sorry about that," he said. "Well, I guess I'd better get back to work on this luau prep."

"We're here to help," Jacob said. "What can we do?"

Uncle Gene sifted through the papers in front of him again and pulled out another list. "Well, now that the mayor and his whole staff are coming to the luau, we need more food! And none of my regular suppliers can deliver on such short notice. Think you can handle it?"

Lana looked over the list. "Definitely!" she said.

Uncle Gene looked relieved.

"Especially with Alfie and Emilia's help," Jacob added.

Alfie thought Emilia had kind of a silly look on her face as she smiled at Jacob, but then again, Jacob had a similar look. "Thanks for letting us try some of the luau food," Emilia said to Uncle Gene.

"Yeah, thank you," Alfie added, popping the rest of his *haupia* into his mouth.

"Absolutely!" Uncle Gene said. "Just wait until you get to try everything at the luau."

Alfie grinned and followed Emilia, Lana, and Jacob out of the kitchen and into the parking lot. He could hardly wait for the luau. Trying new foods had been his favorite part of each adventure, and he knew Maui would be no exception.

Chapter 9

Out in the parking lot, Kai had just finished putting a surfboard in the back of an old pickup truck. Jacob and Lana ran toward him.

"Uncle Gene needs our help," Jacob said. "The mayor's coming to the luau!"

"Whoa," Kai responded. "What does he need us to do?"

Lana held out the list Uncle Gene had given them. "He gave us a list of more food he needs. Can we go pick it up?"

"Definitely," Kai responded, scanning the paper. "We better get going. It's kind of far."

Kai's truck had an extended cab with two small fold-down seats behind the regular bench seat.

"We'll sit in the back," Lana said, jumping in and buckling her seat belt.

"Are you sure?" Emilia said. "We don't mind sitting back there."

"Nah," Jacob said, folding himself into the tiny seat. "You're the guests. You need to be able to see out, especially on Honoapiilani Highway!"

"Thanks," Alfie said. Zia had been right—Hawaiian people were so friendly and laid-back.

Kai pulled out of the resort parking lot and headed down the street. They passed a few strip malls and scuba-gear stores before reaching a neighborhood with small houses lining each side of the road.

"The town the resort is in is called Lahaina," Kai told them. "Jacob and Lana will have to take you to old Lahaina. It used to be the center of government for Hawaii a long time ago. There's some cool history here."

"I love history!" Emilia said.

"Me too!" Jacob added from the back.

"Really?" Emilia asked, turning around to smile at Jacob. Alfie rolled his eyes.

Before long they were picking up speed as the road turned into a highway and carried them close to the water.

"Is this Hono . . . ?" Emilia started. Alfie couldn't remember the name Jacob had said, either.

"Honoapiilani," Jacob and Lana said together.

"Just watch the water as we drive," Kai said.

Alfie and Emilia peered out the driver's-side window to the wide expanse of ocean that was right beside the road. Alfie could see another of the Hawaiian Islands off in the distance. Picturing one of the maps on his bedroom wall, he guessed that was Lanai. "What are we looking for?" he asked. But as soon as the words escaped his lips, he saw it. First, a puff of mist sprayed up from the surface, then a dark mass arched through the water before flipping its giant tail and disappearing again.

"A whale!" Emilia cried.

"Whoa," Alfie whispered. "That was so cool."

"I can't believe we can see whales as we're driving on the highway!" Emilia said. "That's crazy!"

"That's Maui." Kai smiled.

"You guys are here at the perfect time," Lana said. "It's peak season for whale watching right now."

"What kind of whales are they?" Emilia asked.

"Humpback whales," Lana replied. "They swim all the way from Alaska to breed off the coast of Hawaii."

"And this exact spot—on the west shore of Maui—is one of the best places for whale watching in the world," Jacob added.

"That's so awesome!" Alfie replied. He couldn't believe their luck—or maybe it was Zia's incredible timing.

They watched the ocean for a bit longer and saw a few more spouts and one whale that launched halfway out of the water before splashing into the sea again. They could hardly believe what they were seeing!

Pretty soon, the highway turned away from the water and headed inland.

"Now we're driving north to the other side of the island," Jacob said from the backseat.

"Yeah, we're going Upcountry," Lana added.

"What's that?" Alfie asked.

"Upcountry is the inland area of Maui at the base of the Haleakala Crater," Kai explained.

"Is that one of the volcanoes?" Alfie asked.

"Yep," Kai said.

"Cool," Alfie replied as they drove up a winding road into the green rolling hills.

"It's so beautiful," Emilia said.

Alfie nodded in agreement. He was glad they were getting to see what the island looked like away from the resort. He saw kids playing in yards as they wound their way up the twisty road. He smiled. "It would be so fun to grow up on an island like this."

Kai smiled back. "It is. We spend most of our time outside."

Soon Kai clicked his right turn signal and slowed in front of a big sign.

"'Ohi Farm,'" Alfie read aloud.

"*Ohi* means to gather or pick up," Lana said. "This is

an organic fruit farm where they let you pick your own if you want."

Kai swung the truck into a dirt parking lot, and they all piled out of the cab. Alfie stretched his legs. It was a longer drive than he'd expected.

Alfie and Emilia followed their friends around the side of a big building. There was a covered area set up with several large wooden tables piled high with different kinds of fruit. Alfie breathed deep, sniffing the sweetness of various fruits in the air. Emilia smiled and closed her eyes, smelling the fruit, too.

When Alfie stepped up to one of the tables, he scanned the fruit in front of him, looking for anything that was familiar. He could only pick out a couple of things that he recognized. He saw pineapples, mangoes, and pomegranates, but the rest were a mystery!

"Good afternoon," the woman behind the table said. "Let me know what you'd like to try. You're welcome to sample anything we have."

"Thank you," Emilia said. "I guess I don't know what a lot of these fruits are."

"That's okay!" The woman smiled. "We have got a lot of exotic varieties. I'll cut a few things for you."

Alfie and Emilia watched as she picked up a bright red oval-shaped fruit with flat green spikes growing out of the sides. She cut the fruit in half. The inside was white with little black seeds. Alfie was surprised. He hadn't known what to expect, but he hadn't expected it to look so strange inside!

The woman cut two small cubes from the inside and handed them to Alfie and Emilia. "This is dragon fruit," she said.

The flesh was crunchy and easy to bite, with a mild sweetness to it. It was really good!

Alfie decided he liked dragon fruit.

Next the woman carefully picked up a spiky yellow fruit the size of a volleyball.

"That looks dangerous!" Emilia said.

Jacob, Lana, Kai, and the woman all laughed. "You definitely have to be careful handling it," the woman said.

"What is it?" Alfie asked.

"This is durian," the woman replied. "Have you heard of durian before?"

Alfie and Emilia shook their heads.

"I'm going to stand over here for this one," Kai said, moving away from the table. Alfie turned to see Jacob and Lana backing up, too. He couldn't imagine why they'd be scared of a piece of fruit—although it did look a little dangerous . . .

"It can be a bit of an acquired taste," the woman said, using a sharp knife to cut lengthwise across the fruit between rows of spikes.

Alfie frowned. He'd already heard that about the poi.

He glanced at Emilia, and she didn't look so sure, either.

Next the woman used her hands to pry the two halves of the durian husk apart, revealing yellowish flesh inside with big pits in each half. And that's when Alfie smelled it. It smelled like stinky cheese or sweaty gym socks—or a combination of the two; either way, it wasn't exactly something he wanted to put in his mouth. Emilia was already backing away from the table to join their Hawaiian friends, who were laughing, but from a pretty big distance.

"Are you going to try it?" Alfie asked Emilia. She pinched her nose and shook her head.

"What about you?" the woman asked, holding out a spoonful of the fleshy fruit. Alfie took a deep breath. He hadn't shied away from trying anything new on their travels, and he certainly didn't want to now. Alfie took the spoon and shoved it into his mouth before he could change his mind. The durian was slightly creamy and very soft. It tasted kind of like custard, but had more of a strong stinky-cheese aftertaste. Alfie swallowed quickly and made a face. He'd done it, but he wouldn't be going back for more.

Jacob and Kai laughed and clapped from several tables away.

"Bravo!" Kai cheered.

The woman behind the table laughed, too. "We can move to another table and try a couple of other things if you want."

"Yes, please," Alfie said, swiftly joining his friends. He definitely needed to try more fruit to get the cheesy taste out of his mouth.

After that, the woman cut star fruit, rose apple, and jackfruit, which were all interesting and really tasty— much better than the durian. When they were finished, Jacob pulled out Uncle Gene's list and handed it to the woman. She disappeared into the building. A few minutes later she returned with two big wooden crates brimming with fresh tropical fruit.

"I'll put it on the resort's tab," she said. "Enjoy the luau!"

Kai led the way to the truck, and they slid the crates into the back. They thanked the woman and climbed inside. Emilia still looked like she might be sick from the durian smell. Kai started the engine, and they turned onto the road again. Emilia rolled down the window and stuck her head out.

"You're quite the adventurer," Kai said to Alfie.

Alfie beamed. Kai was right—Alfie was up for anything. He just hoped he could get rid of that durian aftertaste eventually!

Chapter 10

They continued on the winding Upcountry road for a few more miles. Then Kai pulled off the road and through two big open wooden gates. An archway over the gates read HOKU RANCH.

"I never imagined there would be ranches in Hawaii," Emilia said.

Alfie nodded. He thought ranches only existed in places like Colorado and Montana.

"Absolutely," Kai said. "Hawaii has a long history of cattle ranching. This ranch even raises elk."

"Elk?" Alfie said. That was even harder to imagine!

"Yep," Jacob said as they climbed out of the truck.

"They make really good elk burgers."

Kai went into the ranch store to get the extra meats Uncle Gene needed for the luau while Lana, Jacob, Alfie, and Emilia stood at the edge of the pasture fence and watched some cattle grazing on a hill nearby. Clouds covered the sun for a few minutes, and Alfie felt a couple of raindrops on his face. But just as quickly, the sun came out again and the rain disappeared.

"What does elk meat taste like?" Emilia asked.

"It's a little like venison, if you've ever had that," Jacob answered. "I bet they'd give you a taste of elk burger in the store if you want."

"Okay, sure!" Emilia said. She'd tried most of the adventurous foods they'd been offered on their travels—like chicken's feet in Hong Kong and alligator tail in New Orleans. She could be just as daring as Alfie.

Jacob led Emilia into the store to try the elk burger. Alfie and Lana followed them inside. Kai was at the counter talking to one of the ranch workers when Jacob appeared at his side to ask about the elk.

"Just a small taste," Emilia told them. The man behind the counter smiled and nodded and went back to the kitchen. He returned a few minutes later with a couple bites of a grilled burger patty on a paper plate.

"Thank you," Emilia said as she picked up a piece of the elk burger and chewed it slowly. "It's good!" she said. "It tastes a little richer and sweeter than a hamburger."

Jacob grabbed the other piece from the plate and

popped it into his mouth. *"Mahalo,"* he said to the man behind the counter.

"What does *mahalo* mean?" Emilia asked.

"It means *thank you*," Jacob told her.

Two men emerged from the back of the store carrying a large cooler. Kai grabbed a second, smaller cooler from the counter and led the way out to the truck.

"Uncle Gene must have ordered another pig to roast," Lana said. "This luau is going to be big!"

Kai and the men slid the coolers into the back next to the fruit crates. Then Emilia and Alfie and their Hawaiian friends all piled into the cab and were on their way. They headed down from the Upcountry and back onto one of the main highways. Alfie read the names of roads and businesses as they drove. "A lot of the names of things seem really similar," he observed.

"That's because the Hawaiian alphabet only has thirteen letters." Jacob leaned over the backseat of the truck.

"Really?"

"Yeah. The Hawaiian language was never written down until British explorers and missionaries came here. Then they recorded it."

"Wow," Emilia said. Alfie could tell she was interested in hearing more about Hawaiian history—especially if it came from Jacob.

After they drove for a while longer, Kai pulled into a convenience-store parking lot. "Who needs a snack?"

"I do!" Jacob called from the back. Alfie agreed. They hadn't really had any lunch. The fruit had been delicious—well, except for the durian—but it hadn't filled him up.

Alfie and Emilia followed their friends into the roadside store and looked around. For the most part, it looked like any convenience store they'd see back home. There were rows of chips and candy and coolers of drinks. But Lana, Jacob, and Kai weren't interested in that stuff. Alfie walked up to the counter to see what they were getting.

"Five Spam *musubis*, please," Jacob told the man behind the counter. "You have to try one," Jacob said to Alfie and Emilia.

Alfie dug in his pocket to give Jacob the couple of dollars he had left after the resort store, but Jacob just waved him away.

"Our treat," he said.

"Thank you!" Alfie and Emilia both said.

They headed to a picnic table outside the convenience store and sat down to eat their snack.

"How long are you two here for?" Kai asked.

Alfie looked at Emilia. "Oh, you know, a few days, I think . . . ," he stumbled.

"We're going to one of the other islands after this," Emilia jumped in. "We're just not sure when exactly."

"Oh, cool," Jacob said. "Which one?"

Emilia gave Alfie a purposeful look. He knew she was hoping he'd remember the other island names from all his map studying. "Uh . . . Oahu?"

"Nice!" Kai responded. "You'll definitely have to check out the North Shore on Oahu. That's where all the crazy surfing competitions are. The waves are insane."

"Awesome!" Alfie said. Now he wished they really were going to Oahu!

Jacob removed the plastic wrap from his Spam *musubi*. "You've had Spam before, right?"

"No . . ." Alfie and Emilia shook their heads.

"Really?" Jacob asked with wide eyes. "Spam is *so delicious*. You definitely can't come to Hawaii without trying it."

"We Hawaiians love our Spam." Lana laughed.

"What . . . what is it?" Emilia asked tentatively.

"*Spam* stands for *spiced ham*," Kai said. "It comes in a can. It got popular during World War II when a lot of soldiers were stationed here."

"Canned ham?" Alfie asked. He was intrigued.

"So Spam *musubi* is kind of like a Hawaiian-slash-Japanese snack because it's served almost like sushi," Kai continued. "It's a ball of rice with a piece of fried Spam on top and wrapped in nori, which is seaweed."

"It does look like a big piece of sushi," Emilia said.

"That's another cool thing about Hawaii," Jacob said. "We are a mix of a lot of different cultures. Hawaiian culture comes from all the other cultures that have settled here: Polynesian, Japanese, Filipino, even Portuguese."

"That is cool," Emilia said. "It's not like anywhere else in the United States."

"Totally," Alfie agreed. He was ready to try his Spam snack. He unwrapped it and took a big bite. The ham was greasy and salty. The consistency wasn't like any ham he'd ever had—it was almost spongy, but he really liked it.

"What do you think?" Kai asked.

"It's really different, but it's good!" Alfie said.

"Emilia?"

"It's pretty good!" Emilia answered, chewing her bite.

"Now you can definitely say you've experienced

Hawaiian culture," Jacob said.

Alfie thought he could see Emilia's cheeks get pink as she smiled at Jacob.

He finished his snack in just a few more bites. "I wonder what Zia would think of Spam," he said to Emilia. "Do you think she tried it when she lived here?"

Emilia laughed. "Good question. I bet she did."

"Yeah." Alfie nodded. Alfie knew Zia would happily try local foods anywhere she visited. That must be where he got his own sense of food adventure.

Chapter 11

Back at the resort, Alfie and Emilia carried one of the crates of fruit into the kitchen. Uncle Gene and Pika were arguing again but stopped abruptly when they realized they had company.

"How did it go?" Uncle Gene asked, attempting a smile, but looking even more frazzled than when they had left. Pika sighed loudly and stormed off to the walk-in freezer.

"No problems at all!" Kai said.

"Good," Uncle Gene said. He turned to Alfie and Emilia. "Did you have fun?"

"We did!" Emilia answered. "The Upcountry was beautiful."

"And I tried durian at the fruit farm," Alfie announced.

"You did?" Uncle Gene looked really surprised. Even one of dishwashers stopped working and looked at Alfie.

"It was disgusting, but I tried it!"

Uncle Gene threw his head back and laughed. "Good for you! It's always good to try new things."

"That's what our *zia* always says," Alfie replied.

Uncle Gene looked like he was going to ask Alfie a question, but Kai spoke first. "I think you've earned yourself another surf lesson, bro—even just for trying that durian today!"

"Sweet!" Alfie said.

Kai smiled. "Well, I've got some other lessons scheduled this afternoon, but I have an opening tomorrow morning if you want to meet me down at the beach at eight o'clock."

"I'll be there!" Alfie replied, excitement building in his chest again. He couldn't wait to get back out on a surfboard.

"I'll come down in the morning, too," Lana said to Emilia. "We can do hula then."

"Great!" Emilia answered. Alfie knew she was as excited about learning to hula dance as he was about surfing.

"Well, I better get back to dealing with this luau," Uncle Gene said, glancing in Pika's direction. "I just hope we can pull it all together."

Jacob patted his uncle's arm. "You can do it!"

"Thanks again for your help, kids," Uncle Gene said. "Now go have fun!"

"Are you sure?" Lana asked.

"Yes," Uncle Gene said. "I think we can take it from here."

Alfie heard Pika mumble something as he walked by, but he couldn't make it out.

"Bye, Uncle Gene!" they all called as they filed out of the kitchen and back into the parking lot. Kai waved good-bye as he headed down to the beach for his next lesson.

"What are you guys doing now?" Jacob asked.

Alfie and Emilia looked at each other and shrugged.

"Want to go snorkeling or paddleboarding?" Jacob asked.

"Sure!"

"We can borrow gear from the resort's rental cabana," Lana said, walking toward the path to the beach. "Kai won't mind."

They hurried down the path to the cabana, and Lana and Jacob went inside. Alfie watched Kai giving his surf lesson out in the water. He couldn't wait until tomorrow!

Lana and Jacob emerged from the cabana, with a couple of net bags of snorkel gear and two paddleboards with paddles.

"We have to walk a little ways to the cove from here," Jacob said. "But it's worth it."

Alfie grabbed one of the boards from Jacob. "Sounds good."

Emilia frowned at him. "I want to try paddleboarding," she said.

"Okay," Alfie huffed. "We'll figure it out when we get there."

Emilia opened her mouth to argue again, but then changed her mind. She took one of the net snorkeling bags from Lana.

They walked down the beach away from the resort. Alfie kicked off his flip-flops, ready to feel the warm, soft sand on his toes again. "Is all the sand in Hawaii like this?" he asked.

"Nope," Lana said. "All the beaches are different. Some have really coarse yellow sand. Others even have black sand."

"Black sand?" Alfie asked.

"Yeah," Lana continued. "Black sand is made from volcanic lava rocks. The rocks get worn down over time."

"That's really cool," Alfie said.

After a while of walking on the beach, they followed a path up and away from the water that went around a rocky point.

"It sounded like Uncle Gene and Pika were fighting again," Jacob said to Lana as they walked.

Lana sighed. "I know. They just can't seem to get along lately."

Alfie glanced at Emilia, hearing his dad's words about the two of them.

"I just want everything to go smoothly for Uncle Gene," Jacob continued. "This luau is a really big deal for him."

Lana nodded. "He could become the chef that the mayor uses for all his parties!"

On the other side of the rocky point, the path curved back down to the sand and into a cove. There were people spread out all down the beach, sunning on the sand, and there were several people snorkeling and paddleboarding in the cove. Alfie breathed in the ocean air as he took in the scene and smiled. He didn't think he ever wanted to leave!

They found a spot on the sand, and Lana and Jacob

helped each other separate out the snorkel gear. They laughed and chatted as they worked.

"Who wants to paddleboard with me?" Jacob asked.

"I do!" Emilia said instantly, looking at Alfie.

He held up his hands in surrender. "Fine." He didn't feel like arguing again just now.

"You'll love snorkeling," Lana told Alfie. "This cove is perfect for it since there aren't big waves. We might even see a sea turtle."

Alfie perked up. That sounded pretty cool.

He watched as Jacob helped Emilia get steady on her stand-up board. Then he showed her how to paddle in the water, and soon they were headed out into the calm surf. Alfie and Lana stood in the shallow water, and Lana demonstrated how to put on the face mask and breathing tube. She led the way into the water and pointed out where Alfie should be careful of coral.

The minute Alfie put his face under the water, he was amazed at the marine life. Bright blue and yellow fish darted in and out of the coral reefs and all around him. Lana was a great guide, directing him toward different fish as they swam around the cove. After a while, Lana pointed excitedly in front of her. Alfie swam alongside, and a big sea turtle came into view. Its black legs and head were covered in patterns that made its skin look like it was cracked all over. Its lighter shell was covered in neat diamond and octagon shapes. It was beautiful. Lana and Alfie followed the sea turtle for a long time. When it started swimming into deeper water, they turned back and headed for the shore. They came up onto the sand and looked around for Jacob and Emilia. They were paddling back in.

Alfie took off his mask to talk to Lana about how cool the sea turtle was, but she was looking down the beach with a frown on her face. Jacob pulled his board up onto the beach and stood next to Lana.

Alfie followed their gazes down the sand. There was a group of people gathered around something taking pictures. A young kid in the group was moving in close to touch it. "What's going on?" Alfie asked.

"There's a sea turtle on the beach," Lana told him. "And those tourists are getting way too close."

"We'd better go over there and tell them to move back," Jacob said.

Lana nodded. Alfie could read the concern on both of their faces. "Alfie and Emilia, can you go to the parking area and see if you can find a Parks Department person to help us?"

"Sure," Emilia said.

Lana dropped her snorkel gear on top of the net bag, and she and Jacob took off down the beach.

Alfie and Emilia hurried up a path that led to the edge of a parking area. Emilia scanned the lot. "It looks like that woman is wearing a uniform. Let's ask her."

They rushed over to the woman. Her green shirt said DEPARTMENT OF PARKS AND RECREATION on it.

"Excuse me, ma'am," Emilia said. "There's a sea turtle on the beach, and people are getting really close to it."

"Okay," the woman said. "Show me where."

They dashed back down to the beach. Jacob and Lana were talking to the crowd of tourists and gesturing toward a posted sign that warned visitors to keep a distance from sea life. Several of the people had started to back away.

The parks worker quickly used pieces of driftwood and rocks on the beach to create a wide barrier around the sea turtle, with an open path allowing it to get back to the water easily. "This is how much space sea turtles, seals, and other animals need when they wander up onto the beach," the woman told the crowd. "It's very important to keep your distance and respect the wildlife here on Maui."

The people nodded and asked the woman a few questions. They took more pictures—but from around the barrier—

and then went back to their other beach activities.

"Thanks for your help, kids," the parks woman said. "That was quick thinking."

"We're just glad we got back to the beach when we did," Lana said.

The four friends went to pick up their gear where they'd left it. There was a slight coolness to the breeze now, and the sun wasn't as high in the sky. As they carried the gear back toward the resort, Alfie felt a few drops of rain hit his face again, and he saw a rainbow form beyond the rocky point. Zia was right—Maui was breathtaking.

Alfie's legs were heavy in the sand. He felt tired from their eventful day. But that wouldn't keep him from his surf lesson the next morning!

Chapter 12

Alfie peeked his eyes open and stared across the darkened room. Emilia had drawn the curtains closed over the balcony windows the night before, even though Alfie had fought to keep them open. It was an argument that he was too tired to try to win at the time. But now his annoyance was renewed as he had no idea what time it was!

He scooted to the edge of his bed, which took some doing considering how big it was. Then he rushed over to the windows and flung open the curtains. Now he could see the clock on the desk, which told him it was 7:15 a.m. He slid open the glass door and stepped onto the balcony, breathing in huge lungfuls of the salty morning air. He glanced down at the beach and saw a couple of surfers dotting the water. He was ready to get out there.

He went back inside and peeked into Emilia's room. She was squinting awake. Alfie launched himself onto her bed. "Let's go! Let's go!" he said as he bounced.

Emilia threw a pillow at him. "Stop bouncing."

Alfie jumped off the bed and ran to the bathroom to get his board shorts. Two seconds later, he came out of the bathroom dressed and ready to go.

"Let's go!" he chanted again.

"Give me a minute," Emilia said, still rubbing her eyes and trying to wake up.

"We said we'd be down there by eight," Alfie argued.

"I know," Emilia growled. "We have plenty of time!"

Alfie sighed and went back out to the balcony. He was frustrated that he and Emilia still couldn't seem to get along. Finally, he heard the bathroom door close and knew Emilia was at least getting ready.

Finally, Emilia emerged. Alfie grabbed their towels and headed for the door.

"What about breakfast?" Emilia asked. "I'm hungry."

Alfie stopped. That was a good point. And now that he thought about it, he was hungry, too. "We could order room service!" he said. Visions of Belgian waffles and fluffy omelets delivered on a rolling cart filled his mind.

Emilia shook her head. "Then they might see that no one is actually supposed to be in this room."

Alfie chewed on the inside of his lip and thought. "Hey, maybe that buffet is set up in the courtyard again. We could grab something from there."

Emilia hesitated but finally said, "Okay."

Alfie put the key card in his pocket and followed Emilia into the hall. As they waited for the elevator, a family joined them, smiling and saying hello. Once they were down on the ground floor, the family exited first, so Alfie and Emilia followed behind. The family went straight out to the courtyard, where a long buffet table piled with food was set up.

Alfie grinned at Emilia. They stayed close to the family as they passed a resort employee. But once outside, Alfie split away and walked the length of the table, staring at all the tasty food. There were dishes full of bacon and sausages, scrambled eggs and potatoes, fried rice, smoked salmon, and even poi. Alfie wanted to fill a plate and eat until he was stuffed, but he knew they didn't have time—not to mention that there was no way he'd be able to surf after eating all that food.

Just then Emilia tugged at his T-shirt sleeve and nodded her head toward a waiter at the end of the table. He asked the family for their room number and the last name on their room and wrote it down. "We'd better go," Emilia said.

"Yeah," Alfie agreed. But not before he grabbed two muffins and a banana from the end of the table. They dashed back into the lobby and ducked behind a pillar. Alfie handed one of the muffins to Emilia.

"Thanks," she said. "Do you think he saw us?"

Alfie peered out from behind the pillar. A man in khaki pants and a Hawaiian shirt was smiling down at him. "Good morning," the man said. His name tag said FRANK, MANAGER.

"Hi," Alfie replied quietly.

"Are you looking for your parents?" Frank asked.

"Um, yeah. I think they're out at the pool already, though. We'll just go check." Alfie started toward the side door.

"No problem," Frank replied. "If they aren't there, I'd be happy to page them. Just let me know."

"Okay, we will," Emilia added, shoving Alfie toward the door.

Frank watched them walk outside, but when Alfie peered back in through the glass, he noticed that the manager had moved on to talking to a couple who had just arrived. Alfie turned to Emilia and took a giant bite of his muffin. "All clear," he said as crumbs fell from his mouth.

Emilia frowned. "That was close."

Alfie shrugged in response. "But nothing happened. It's fine. Come on. Aren't you ready for your hula lesson?"

Emilia perked up and peeled the banana, handing half to Alfie. "Yeah. Let's go!"

Kai and Lana were waiting in the rental cabana when Alfie and Emilia got to the beach.

"I hope we're not late," Emilia said.

"Nope, right on time." Lana smiled.

"Where's Jacob?" Emilia asked, her ears turning red.

"Uncle Gene needed his help this morning."

"Oh," Emilia said, looking disappointed.

Alfie was about to tease her when Kai clapped him on the shoulder. "Ready to surf?"

"Definitely!" Alfie pulled off his T-shirt and put on the rash guard Kai held out for him. Then he rushed over to grab his board.

"Emilia, are you sure you don't want to join us?" Kai asked. "You were so good at it yesterday!"

"I'm sure," Emilia said. "I'd really like to learn hula."

"Okay," Kai said. "Have fun."

Lana and Emilia moved over to a grassy area next to the cabana and went to work on their hula moves. Alfie watched Emilia as she concentrated on following Lana's lead. He knew she'd pick up the routine right away. She was a natural at dancing, too. In Rio she had learned the samba for Carnival in no time.

Alfie and Kai paddled out into the surf. Kai hung out behind Alfie's board and helped push him into the surf each time a good wave came. It took him a while, but finally Alfie was catching waves and riding some, too. He couldn't stop smiling as he paddled out to Kai once more.

"Nice work," Kai said. "I'm going to stop pushing your board so you can work on the timing on your own."

"Okay," Alfie said. He was beginning to get the hang of it. And he liked learning to surf more than he'd liked learning the drums. He just wished he could practice this at home!

Kai watched Alfie a little while longer and gave him a few more pointers.

"I'm going to catch some waves, too," Kai said. "Think you can handle it on your own?"

"Sure," Alfie replied.

"There's a junior surf competition being held farther down the beach." Kai pointed off to the right. "But you'll be fine if you stick to this area. I'm going to grab a few of the bigger waves in the other direction, but we'll meet up back at the cabana."

"Okay."

Alfie waited for another wave and managed to ride it all the way in. He watched Kai catch one of the waves in the bigger surf farther down the beach before paddling out again. Alfie let the water carry him a little ways down the shore as he continued to work on his stance and his form.

He was starting to feel kind of tired, so he decided to catch one more wave and then go see how the hula lessons were going. That's when he spotted it—a perfect wave, not too big and not too small. Alfie paddled hard and got on top of it just in time. His timing was perfect, but he was wobbly on his board. He concentrated on just staying upright. Finally, his stance felt more solid. That's when he looked up and realized he'd surfed his way straight into the junior surfing competition!

Chapter 13

Alfie managed to ride the wave all the way in to shore. Before he knew what was happening, people were cheering for him, and the announcer was talking about his form. Metal bleachers were set up in the sand with strings of plastic flags attached to them, blowing in the breeze. A row of people sat at a table under a canopy, and they were all looking at him. Alfie's face flamed red.

He picked up his board and walked out of the shallow water. A woman approached him with a smile on her face.

"I'm sorry, I—" Alfie started to explain.

"Nice work out there," she said. Her T-shirt read WEST MAUI JUNIOR SURF COMPETITION. "You're moving on to the next round of the competition!"

"I am?" Alfie couldn't believe it.

"Looks like you lost your competitor number in the surf, so here's another one." The woman pinned a number onto Alfie's rash guard. "Just be here tomorrow morning at eight thirty for the next round. And good luck!"

"Okay . . . ," Alfie managed.

Alfie walked down the beach with the surfboard under his arm. He started laughing out loud to himself about what had just happened. He had been too focused on what he was doing to realize how far down the beach he'd gone!

Alfie glanced down at the number pinned to his shirt: 426. He laughed again. He couldn't wait to tell Emilia and their new friends what had happened. Kai was going to be proud of him for surfing well enough to qualify. Alfie started to jog with his board. The resort was even farther away than he'd realized, and he was eager to tell his story.

Alfie finally reached the area of beach that was set out with tidy rows of resort chairs and beach umbrellas. He wove his way through them, dodging sunbathers and waiters balancing frozen drinks, and made his way up to the rentals cabana. It looked like Kai had just come in from surfing, too. His surf shirt and board shorts were wet, and he was putting his surfboard away. Emilia and Lana were still on the grass nearby, working on their hula moves. Lana stood slightly in front of Emilia, and Emilia mimicked her moves. They swayed their hips as they stepped lightly on the grass and turned their wrists to make different delicate movements with their hands. As Alfie predicted, Emilia looked like a natural and was following all of Lana's moves with ease.

"Kai!" Alfie shouted. "You're not going to believe it."

But at that moment, Jacob came rushing down the

path toward the cabana. From the look on his face, Alfie could tell something was wrong. His surf story was going to have to wait.

Alfie reached the cabana at the same time as Jacob. He leaned his surfboard against the wall as Emilia and Lana hurried over from the grass.

"What's going on?" Kai asked, also reading their faces.

"Pika and Uncle Gene got in another big argument this morning," Jacob told them. "And Pika quit!"

Lana shook her head. "I can't believe Pika would do that. The luau is tonight!"

"Oh no," Alfie and Emilia said in unison.

Chapter 14

Alfie, Emilia, Jacob, Lana, and Kai all ran up to the resort restaurant to talk to Uncle Gene. When they arrived, Uncle Gene was pacing back and forth, looking completely overwhelmed.

"How could Pika just quit like that?" Lana asked him. "I don't understand."

Uncle Gene sighed. "We haven't been getting along for a while now. We keep arguing over petty things and can't seem to resolve our differences. It just wasn't working out."

Alfie and Emilia exchanged a guilty look.

"It's probably for the best in the long run," Uncle Gene

continued, sweeping some crumbs off the counter. "I just wish he would have waited until after the luau. This is such an important event for the resort, and for me."

Everybody was silent, unsure what to say next. Alfie felt like there was a knot in his stomach. It sounded like Uncle Gene was describing how he and Emilia had been acting, too.

"Well, I guess I'd better get back to work and try to figure out how to pull this off," Uncle Gene said.

"We can help!" Alfie cried.

"Yeah," Emilia added. "Like we said, we've helped in restaurant kitchens before. We can do whatever you need."

Uncle Gene shook his head. "You kids are here on vacation. You should be with your parents. Have you driven the road to Hana yet? Seen the bamboo forest?"

Alfie had to admit a bamboo forest sounded pretty cool, but he knew it was time to step up and support their new friends. "We want to," he said. "It's the least we can do. After all, Kai's surf lessons helped me qualify for a junior surf competition!"

Everybody stared at Alfie with wide eyes. He grinned

from ear to ear as he told the story. Kai laughed extra hard and tugged on the number pinned to Alfie's surf shirt. "If it wasn't for this, I'm not sure I'd even believe you. That's a crazy story!"

"I know!" Alfie beamed. "It still doesn't seem real."

"Way to go, Alfie!" Emilia cried. And Alfie knew she meant it.

"Well, what are we waiting for?" Alfie asked. "We've got a luau to prepare for the mayor!"

Uncle Gene sprang into action. First, he called a meeting of the kitchen staff to let them know that Pika was no longer working at the Grand Lahaina. Then he assigned duties to all of his employees. He and Jacob had already started roasting the pigs in the *imu* earlier that morning, so now it was time to focus on making the other dishes on the menu and preparing the outside space for the festivities.

Uncle Gene made to-do lists for everybody with specific luau tasks. Alfie and Emilia were in charge of cutting up most of the fruit and vegetables while Lana and Jacob were responsible for helping set up the luau dining area. Kai had a few more surf lessons to give, but he promised to come back and pitch in as soon as he was done.

Uncle Gene gave Alfie and Emilia clean aprons to wear and showed them where to wash their hands. They set to work peeling a giant bag of Hawaiian sweet potatoes. They worked in silence for a little while. Then Alfie looked at Emilia across his pile of deep purple sweet potato peels. "I'm sorry I've been fighting with you so much lately. I know I keep starting arguments and making you annoyed."

"I'm sorry, too," Emilia said. "I don't know why I've been so grouchy lately."

"I guess I didn't even realize how bad it was until I heard Uncle Gene talking about his fights with Pika," Alfie continued.

"I know! I felt the same way. It just made me feel bad

thinking about all the dumb fights we've been having—at home and even here."

"Yeah." Alfie looked down at the table. "Well, I promise to be better. Besides, it's so much more fun when we're getting along."

Emilia smiled. "I agree," she said. Then she tossed a potato peel at Alfie. It hung perfectly balanced on the tip of his nose. They both burst out laughing.

Just then, Alfie noticed a man in a suit talking to Uncle Gene in the corner of the kitchen. The man tapped on a tablet as he spoke. Uncle Gene nodded and tried to smile. Soon the man hustled out of the kitchen, now talking on his phone. Uncle Gene's face looked ashen, and he just stared at the countertop.

Alfie wiped his hands on a towel and motioned for Emilia to follow him. "Is everything okay, Uncle Gene?" Alfie asked.

The chef tried to look more composed. "That was the mayor's aide. He wanted to make sure we're serving banana bread at the luau. It's the mayor's favorite."

Alfie nodded, still unsure what the problem was.

"I wasn't going to make banana bread," Uncle Gene continued. "I haven't been able to find a recipe that I really like—not since . . . Well, I used to have a very dear friend here on Maui who made the best banana bread in the world. When she left, it never tasted the same, so I stopped making it." Uncle Gene closed his eyes.

Alfie and Emilia gawked at each other. Alfie was just about to ask Uncle Gene about his "very dear friend" when Lana came into the kitchen.

"We're almost finished setting up outside. It looks great!"

"Very good, Lana," Uncle Gene replied. "Now if I can

just figure out what to do about this banana bread, maybe the whole thing won't be a disaster!"

Alfie had an idea. "We know a recipe," he said. "Our great-aunt makes really good banana bread, and we just helped her the other day."

"That's right!" Emilia said. "We can make it."

Uncle Gene gave Alfie and Emilia a curious look. "Are you sure? We're going to need enough banana bread for a small crowd."

Alfie and Emilia nodded, looking determined. "Yes," Alfie said. "We'll do it."

"Okay," Uncle Gene replied. "Let's see what you've got!"

Alfie and Emilia hurried over to the pantry to get the ingredients they needed. Emilia pulled flour, sugar, brown sugar, salt, baking soda, and baking powder from the shelves.

"We need eggs!" Alfie said. He dashed over to where several cooks were working at the stove and grabbed a carton of eggs.

"What else do we need again?" Emilia asked. "I know we need vanilla and chocolate chips, but there's one more thing…"

"Yogurt!" Alfie shouted, relieved he could remember.

"Yes!" Emilia shouted, giving Alfie a high five. He grinned. It felt much better to be working together than bickering with each other.

"And don't forget the macadamia nuts!" Alfie added.

Emilia started combining the dry ingredients as she'd done at home, while Alfie went to find where the bananas were stored.

One of the cooks pointed him to a bowl piled high with bananas. Alfie grabbed several extra-ripe bunches and hurried back to Emilia's side.

They finished measuring out the rest of the ingredients—enough to make half a dozen loaves—and slowly folded the dry mixture into the wet. Alfie remembered arguing with Emilia about stirring too slowly. Now he just laughed about it.

Chapter 15

Alfie and Emilia anxiously waited for their loaves of banana bread to bake. As soon as the timer went off, they flung open the oven door and slid out the rack with a potholder. Emilia placed a toothpick into the center of each one, and they all pulled out clean. The bread was ready.

Once the bread was cool, Uncle Gene cut a thick slice from one of the loaves, and Lana and Jacob gathered around. Alfie held his breath as their new friends tried the banana bread. Uncle Gene closed his eyes as he chewed. When he opened them, Alfie thought he looked a little teary.

"It's perfect," Uncle Gene whispered. "It tastes just like the banana bread my friend used to make!"

"Yes!" Alfie cheered, giving Emilia a quick hug. They'd done it.

They set the loaves aside to cool and went back to peeling the rest of the sweet potatoes. Now that Uncle Gene knew they had delicious banana bread to serve the mayor, he was in a better mood—even laughing and joking with his kitchen staff as they worked. The rest of the afternoon passed in a flash, and then it was almost time for the luau. Alfie and Emilia finished up by slicing the banana bread and arranging it on big, festive serving trays.

Uncle Gene came over to inspect their work. He put an arm around each of their shoulders and squeezed them into a hug. "You two are *ohana* now. Do you know what that means?"

Alfie and Emilia shook their heads.

"It means you're family," Uncle Gene said. "And you'll

always have a place here with us on Maui."

"Thank you," Emilia said. "That's so nice."

"I'm looking forward to meeting your parents at the luau so I can tell them what remarkable kids they have!" Uncle Gene added.

Alfie and Emilia laughed nervously. "Yeah . . . ," Alfie said.

Just then Lana, Jacob, and Kai hurried over. "We've finished cutting all the fruit, Uncle Gene!" Lana told him. "Everything is set!"

"Wonderful!" Uncle Gene replied. "Now you'd better go get ready for your hula performance, Lana. I think they'll be seating the guests soon."

Lana nodded. "The other dancers are getting ready now. I just thought I'd see if Emilia wanted to join us."

"Me?" Emilia asked.

"You picked up the moves so easily today. I thought it would be fun!" Lana replied. "What do you say?"

"Yes!" Emilia cried. "I say yes!"

"Great. I have a costume for you to wear. Let's go get changed."

Emilia waved excitedly at Alfie as she and Lana ran out of the kitchen. Then Alfie followed Uncle Gene, Jacob, and Kai over to the storage closet to get pants and chef's jackets to put on. Kai was going to be an extra server, and Jacob and Alfie would help run fresh serving trays out to the buffet line. Alfie and Jacob hustled back and forth with the other kitchen staff to set up the buffet table.

Before long, the luau area was full of excited guests, including the mayor and his employees, and a line formed in front of the food. Then Lana and Emilia's hula performance started. Alfie stood off to the side to watch for a few minutes. Emilia wore a big purple skirt and a lighter purple tank top with a shell necklace over it. She had a lei around her head like a crown as well as smaller green wreaths made of palm leaves around her wrists and ankles. She looked super comfortable as she followed

the other dancers through the routine. There were a
few times when Alfie could see she didn't know the next
move, but she handled it well and kept the rhythm of the
dance perfectly. Emilia planned to try out for the dance
team at school next year, and Alfie knew she'd make the
team without a problem.

After the hula performance, the fire dancers performed. Alfie stopped again in between delivering fresh plates to the buffet to watch the amazing dancers move effortlessly as they tossed flaming sticks into the air!

Once the buffet line started to die down, and guests were finishing their meals, Kai told Alfie and Emilia it was their turn to get some food. Alfie was starving after another busy day and couldn't wait to taste all the things they'd been helping to prepare. He and Emilia, Lana, Jacob, and Kai filled plates with all the savory luau foods and sat down at an empty table to the side of the stage to have their meals.

Alfie took a big bite of the shredded *kālua* pork. It was the tastiest meat he'd ever eaten. It was juicy, with the perfect blend of pineapple sweetness and salt. Emilia liked the ahi poke. There were little bright pink chunks of fresh tuna marinated in a citrusy soy sauce with sweet onions.

"I didn't think I would like this," Emilia said. "I've only tried sushi once, and I wasn't sure about it, but this is great."

Alfie scooped up a bite with a crispy taro chip and nodded. "It is really good!"

They also tried thick warm slices of roasted Hawaiian sweet potato and chicken long rice, which was made of shredded chicken and clear noodles in a light broth. The chicken had a yummy ginger taste to it, and the noodles were see-through—almost like they were made of gel!

"I've never seen noodles like this before," Alfie said, taking another bite.

"They're called bean thread or cellophane noodles," Jacob told him.

"I like them," Alfie said.

They even tried poi again, and Alfie had to admit it was a little better when you could eat it along with other, much more flavorful foods. Alfie finished the last piece of shredded pork on his plate just as Lana returned to the table with a plateful of desserts. He smiled. "I was about to say how full I am, but I always have room for dessert!"

Lana laughed. "You don't want to miss this stuff. I got some fresh guava, pineapple, and star fruit. And then these are the *malasadas*," she said, pointing to some balls of fried dough covered in sugar. "They're Portuguese doughnuts, and they're really popular here in Hawaii."

Alfie and Emilia each took a *malasada* from the plate. The fried outside of the dough was still warm and crispy while the inside was soft and delicious. "I feel like there's a different kind of doughnut in every culture in the world," Emilia said.

"That's true!" Alfie replied. "We've had zeppole in Naples, beignets in New Orleans, and now *malasadas* in Hawaii, and they're all different."

Alfie finished his *malasada* and grabbed a couple of pieces of fruit. Then he noticed Uncle Gene talking to the mayor by the dessert table. The mayor was just finishing a slice of their banana bread. Alfie nudged Emilia's side, and they watched as the mayor smiled and shook Uncle Gene's hand. Uncle Gene motioned for him and Emilia to come over.

"Alfie and Emilia, I'd like to introduce you to the mayor of Maui," Uncle Gene said.

"Nice to meet you, Mr. Mayor," Alfie said.

"Gene tells me that you two made this wonderful banana bread," the mayor said.

"Yes, sir," Emilia said.

"Well, this is quite possibly the best banana bread I've ever tasted."

Alfie and Emilia beamed. "Thank you!"

"I'm definitely going to need to get that recipe from you," Uncle Gene said. "I think it's time to bring that back to the menu at the Grand Lahaina."

The mayor nodded. "And you'll definitely need it for all the parties you'll be throwing for the mayor's office."

Uncle Gene beamed. "Absolutely, Mr. Mayor."

Alfie and Emilia smiled. "Enjoy the rest of the luau, Mr. Mayor," Emilia said before they rejoined their friends.

Alfie was full and sluggish as the luau came to an end and he started to help clear the buffet table. Uncle Gene stood at the exit thanking the mayor and the other happy guests as they filed out. Then he came over to thank Alfie and Emilia once more. "I didn't get to meet your parents!" he said. "Are they still here? It would be great to meet them."

"Uh . . . ," Alfie said, unsure how to respond.

"They actually didn't end up coming," Emilia jumped in. "They weren't feeling well, so they stayed in the room. I think they got too much sun on their sightseeing tour today."

Alfie let out a relieved breath. Uncle Gene nodded understandingly. "That happens," he said. "Well, maybe I can meet them tomorrow."

Alfie and Emilia said good night to their friends, and they agreed to meet at the junior surf competition in the morning to cheer Alfie on. They headed across the lobby to the bank of elevators when Frank, the hotel manager, appeared in front of them.

"Did you enjoy the luau?" he asked. He had a friendly smile on his face like yesterday, but his eyes were a little more critical this time.

"We did." Emilia smiled, looking right back. Alfie was surprised at her confidence after she'd been so nervous when they first arrived.

"And what about your parents?" Frank continued.

"Did they have a good time, too?"

"Yep!" Alfie chimed in.

"They just went up to our room early. They were tired," Emilia explained.

"And which room is that?" Frank asked.

Alfie could feel the blood draining from his face. *Oh no!* he thought. This was it!

"It's, um . . . ," Emilia started. "Alfie, what is our room number?"

"It's . . . uh . . . ," Alfie stammered, stalling for time. His heart pounded in his chest.

Suddenly Kai jogged across the lobby toward them. "Hey, Alfie!" he called. He held up the surf shirt Alfie had been wearing before he changed into the kitchen clothes. "Don't forget your number for tomorrow."

"Oh, thanks!" Alfie said, relieved for the interruption. He took the shirt and watched Frank's expression, wondering what they were going to say to get out of giving their room number.

"Hi, Frank," Kai said. "I'm glad you're here. We had a question about where to put the rest of the chairs." Kai motioned for Frank to follow him outside. Frank glanced back at Alfie and Emilia. Emilia smiled and said, "Good night!"

Alfie and Emilia hurried to the elevators without looking back. As soon as the door closed behind them and they were on their way up to suite 1201, they burst out laughing. "That was *really* close this time!" Emilia laughed.

Alfie nodded, catching his breath. Yes, a little too close!

Chapter 16

The minute Alfie and Emilia settled into their giant
beds that night, they were out—totally exhausted from
their eventful day. Alfie had set an alarm so he'd be sure
to wake up on time, but his eyes popped open twenty
minutes before the alarm went off. There was no way he
was going to miss the surfing competition!

Emilia jumped up, too, and got ready quickly so Alfie
wouldn't be late. They took a hurried turn through the
buffet line again and grabbed some breakfast. Out of the
corner of his eye, Alfie spotted Frank greeting a table of
guests, so he and Emilia made a quick getaway down the
path to the beach.

"I don't think we can stay in the suite another night," Emilia said as they hurried toward the water.

"Yeah, me neither," Alfie said, shoving a bite of pineapple in his mouth.

Kai, Lana, Jacob, and even Uncle Gene were waiting for them at the rentals cabana when they arrived. Alfie picked up the lucky surfboard he'd used his last two times out.

"Where are your parents?" Uncle Gene asked, looking around. "I thought for sure they wouldn't want to miss the competition!"

"Oh, right . . . ," Alfie said, shooting Emilia a pleading look for help.

"They're going to meet us over there," she said. "They were slow finishing breakfast, so we went ahead."

Uncle Gene smiled and nodded, looking satisfied with that response.

Alfie had no idea what they were going to do after the competition was over and no parents showed up. But he had more important things to worry about. He was about to surf in a real surfing competition in Maui, Hawaii!

The group made their way down the beach, and Alfie checked in, showing his number to the woman he'd met the day before. She shuffled through her binder, looking embarrassed. "I'm so sorry," she said. "I can't seem to find your name anywhere. Can you remind me what it is?"

"Alfie Bertolizzi," Alfie said proudly.

The woman scribbled it down. "Just head on over to the starting area with the rest of the competitors, and they'll let you know when it's time to paddle out. You'll have three chances to catch a wave."

"Okay . . . ," Alfie said quietly. Suddenly, his nerves were hitting him. What was he doing? He didn't really know how to surf! Maybe he should just forget the whole thing.

Emilia saw his face and grabbed his shoulders. She looked him straight in the eye. "You're going to be great," she said. "Remember everything Kai taught you and just have fun!"

Alfie took a deep breath and nodded. Emilia was right. It wasn't like he'd even known this was going to happen— he should just have fun with it!

Emilia and their new friends cheered at the top of their lungs when Alfie's name was called and he paddled into the surf. He waited for the surfer ahead of him to ride his wave and then got ready to catch his own wave. A wave came and he paddled hard to get on top of it, but he wasn't fast enough, so he treaded water, waiting for another one. Then he saw one that looked perfect. Even over the rushing sound of the water, he thought he heard Kai yelling at him to go for it. So Alfie dug his arms into the water, paddling fast. He felt the wave behind him and popped up into a solid stance. He wavered several times, but stayed upright on the board. He even managed a slight turn as he rode the wave into shallow water.

He heard his name called over the intercom system again, and the crowd clapped for him. He felt great! And more importantly, it was fun.

They waited for a few more surfers to finish the round, and then the judges tallied the scores. Alfie's score wasn't high enough to qualify him for the next round, but he didn't care. After all, it was only the third time he'd ever surfed! The contest organizer came over and held out an envelope to Alfie. "Thanks for competing!" she said.

Inside the envelope was a ribbon with WEST MAUI JUNIOR SURF COMPETITION PARTICIPANT written on it and fifty dollars in cash!

Uncle Gene gave Alfie a big hug. "Way to go!" he said. Then he pulled Emilia in for a hug, too. "I should get back up to the kitchen. Thank you both again for your help with the luau. I couldn't have done it without you and your amazing banana bread recipe."

"We loved it. It was really fun!" Emilia said.

"Good. And don't forget, you're *ohana* now." Uncle Gene smiled and waved as he headed back to the resort.

Next Kai pulled Alfie under his arm and ruffled his dark hair with his fist. "Nice job, bro. I still can't believe you did that!"

"Thanks." Alfie grinned.

"I gotta go get ready," Kai said. "I've got back-to-back lessons today."

"We'll come help you this afternoon," Jacob told Kai. "We thought we'd take Alfie and Emilia to old Lahaina town first."

"You guys have done so much for us already," Emilia said. "Are you sure you can spare the time?"

"Absolutely," Jacob said, looking at Emilia with soft eyes. "We're happy to."

Alfie saw that Emilia was blushing again.

They walked back to the resort and hopped on a shuttle bus to take them to the center of town.

It was a short ride on the shuttle bus, and soon they were pulling up to the old town square.

"Whoa. Look at that tree!" Alfie cried as he stepped out onto the sidewalk. The entire town square was shaded by an enormous tree with branches extending out in all directions. There were even sections where more roots had sprouted from branches and anchored to the ground away from the main trunk. It was the biggest, coolest-looking tree Alfie had ever seen.

"That's the banyan tree," Lana told him. "It was brought all the way from India in the late eighteen hundreds."

"And it's been here ever since?" Alfie asked.

"Yep."

They walked under the giant branches of the banyan tree. Alfie turned in circles looking at it from all angles.

"Like Kai said before, this used to be the center of the Hawaiian government back in the eighteen hundreds," Jacob said. "People came here from all over the world—especially because of the whaling they used to do."

Emilia looked stricken. "But they don't hunt whales anymore, right?"

"Definitely not!" Jacob said. "Now the big business is whale watching." He gestured across the street at the row of sandwich boards advertising all the different whale-watching trips you could take from the Lahaina pier.

"Hey, we should get some fish tacos from that little stand," Lana suggested. "Does that sound good?"

"Yes!" Alfie replied instantly. He had definitely worked up an appetite after surfing that morning.

They crossed the street and found a vendor selling fresh mahimahi tacos. Lana and Jacob ordered two tacos with a dollop of pineapple salsa on top for each of them.

"Wait!" Alfie said, digging in the pocket of his board shorts. He pulled out the envelope with his surf winnings in it and handed some cash to Lana.

"That's okay," Lana said.

"No, please," Alfie replied. "You guys have done so much for us. We have to be able to thank you somehow!"

Jacob and Lana smiled. "Thanks!"

The four friends sat on a bench under the banyan tree while they enjoyed their tacos. The fish was so fresh, Alfie wouldn't have been surprised if it had been caught that morning. After a while, Lana stood up. "I guess we should head back to the resort and help Kai with all the lessons he has booked this afternoon. Are you guys coming?"

Alfie looked at the boats across the street. "We might

try to do a whale-watching trip first."

"You definitely should," Lana said.

"Will we see you back at the resort?" Jacob asked, catching Emilia's eye.

"Maybe...," Alfie said. He really wasn't sure if they'd make it past Frank again or when their adventure might be coming to an end.

"I hope so," Emilia added. "But if not, thank you both again for everything. We've had such a great time." Emilia hugged Lana and then hesitated before hugging Jacob. Her cheeks were bright red.

"Okay," Lana said. "Well, hopefully we'll see you later."

"*Mahalo!*" Alfie called as Lana and Jacob headed across the square where a resort shuttle was loading up.

Alfie looked at Emilia, unsure what to say. He thought she looked sad. "I know something that will cheer you up," he said finally.

"What?" she asked.

He led the way down the street past the fish taco

vendor to another vendor he'd spotted earlier. It was a cart selling Hawaiian shave ice. Alfie gestured toward the cart, and Emilia smiled. "Okay, you're right," she said.

"Two rainbow flavors, please," Alfie told the man.

"Would you like a scoop of ice cream in the bottom of your cup?" the man asked.

"Yes, please!" Alfie said. "Even better."

The man handed back two cups overflowing with ice shaved off a large block and colored in a rainbow of blue, red, yellow, and green. Alfie paid with his surf money, and they headed toward the waterfront to watch whales while they enjoyed their frozen treat.

Alfie crunched on a raspberry- flavored icy bite. "This has been a pretty incredible trip," he said.

"It has," Emilia responded. "I'm going to have a lot to write about in my journal when we get home."

Alfie smiled. He'd gotten Emilia a journal for her birthday to write about all their adventures. It made him happy to think of all the pages she'd be able to fill in from their time in Hawaii.

"I wonder when we'll be going back home," Alfie said between bites.

"Good question," Emilia said. "We should definitely do one of the whale-watching tours today. It would make up for the disastrous one we took a few summers ago. Remember?"

Alfie almost spit out his bite of shave ice. "I remember. The water was so choppy, and we were all seasick. I swear Mom's face was green!"

"Yeah, like the color of this shave ice," Emilia added.

Alfie laughed and took another bite. Just then he felt the air shift around him, and his stomach did a flip— almost like being on a boat in the waves . . .

Chapter 17

Alfie blinked a few times, and his eyes came into focus on Zia in their kitchen.

"I know we've just made banana bread, but I thought we could make some popcorn and watch a movie," Zia said, smiling at them with a bit of a twinkle in her eye.

Alfie looked at Emilia and exchanged a grin.

Zia added vegetable oil and popcorn kernels to a large, heavy pot on the stove. "Emilia, would you mind grabbing a TV tray from the garage?" Zia asked.

"I'll do it!" Alfie offered.

"Thanks," Emilia said, opening the garage door for Alfie. "Let me know if you need any help."

When Alfie came back into the kitchen with the TV tray, Zia just stood and stared at him and Emilia.

"What?" Emilia laughed.

"It's just that you two seem to be getting along much better," Zia said, still looking surprised.

"We are," Alfie told her. "All thanks to you!"

"Me?" Zia asked. "What did I do?"

"We had the best time in Maui, Zia," Emilia said. "I learned to hula dance, Alfie learned to surf, we helped with a luau ..."

"And made new friends," Alfie added.

Zia laughed as she removed the pot of freshly popped popcorn from the stove and transferred it to a bowl, sprinkling salt over the top. "I just love that you both have such vivid imaginations."

"Zia!" Alfie and Emilia both cried.

Zia winked at them and picked up the bowl of popcorn and some napkins. Alfie and Emilia followed her into the family room.

"Now I definitely know what state to write my history report on—Hawaii."

"Oh?" Zia asked.

"It's just so unique and diverse—all those cultures coming together to create such cool foods and traditions. I think it's the most interesting state in the whole country."

"But you haven't visited them all yet," Alfie said, grabbing a handful of popcorn.

"That's true," Emilia said. "There are a lot of states I haven't even seen ..."

"I guess we just need to keep going on adventures, then," Alfie said, grinning at Zia.

Zia nodded. "Visiting new places is the best way to learn and grow in all areas of your life. Each time you travel, you not only learn something about a new place, you learn something about yourself."

Alfie and Emilia were quiet for a minute as they thought about this. Zia was totally right! They'd learned a ton of stuff about Maui and Hawaiian culture, but they'd also learned how important it was for them to get along and work together.

"I've learned how much I like surfing!" Alfie said, breaking the thoughtful mood.

Zia and Emilia laughed. "Well, in honor of your newfound love of surfing, I have the perfect movie for us to watch," Zia said.

"Really?" Alfie asked. "What is it?"

"It's called *The Endless Summer*," Zia told him. "It's a fantastic surf documentary from the sixties, and it's one of my favorite movies of all time."

"Is it filmed in Hawaii?" Emilia asked.

"Part of it. It follows a group of surfers around the world in search of the best waves and the best weather."

"That sounds awesome!" Alfie said. "What are we waiting for?"

Zia laughed again. "The DVD should be in the cabinet."

Alfie hopped off the sofa and skidded over to the TV cabinet. He searched through a couple of stacks of DVDs and finally found *The Endless Summer*. He opened the DVD case, and tucked inside was a small photo. Alfie pulled the photo out of the case and held it up. It was Zia from many years ago. She was posing on the beach in a bathing suit. A tall Hawaiian man stood next to her with his arm around her shoulder, pulling her into a hug. His other arm was arched around a surfboard that stood upright in the sand. He had a big, friendly smile and warm dark eyes. Alfie stared at the photo a while longer. The man next to Zia looked like a younger version of Uncle Gene—he was sure of it!

Alfie jumped up from the carpet and ran over to the sofa where Zia and Emilia sat. "Look!" he said, showing them the photo.

"Is that . . . ?" Emilia started to ask with wide eyes.

"It's Uncle Gene!" Alfie said, unable to control his excitement. "It has to be!"

"You were friends with Uncle Gene?" Emilia asked, getting just as excited as Alfie. "He was so nice, Zia. We loved him!"

"Yeah, and he told us we are *ohana*," Alfie added.

Zia stood up and went over to the DVD player. She slid the disc into the machine and returned to the sofa. A smile was beginning to form on the edges of her lips. "Such vivid imaginations," she said finally.

"Zia!" Alfie and Emilia protested again.

Zia settled on the sofa between Alfie and Emilia, and put the bowl of popcorn on her lap. The movie started, and Alfie was soon swept away by the amazing surfers and their quest. But he couldn't help sneaking an occasional glance at Zia, wondering where their next adventure might take them.

A Note from Giada

There is something about Hawaii . . . for one thing, it's the food, with its bright, sweet, exotic fruits, and its savory dishes like slow-roasted *kālua* pork, lomi lomi salmon, and, of course, poi! But more than that, it's the feeling I get when I'm there. The sun is big and bright, the people are so happy and friendly, the air is clean and pure. When you live in Los Angeles like I do, it's a very quick trip to Hawaii, and I love hopping over there to relax, surf, swim in the ocean, and even snorkel and see all the beautiful, vibrant fish.

One thing that I really love is all the "aloha"s you hear while you're there. It's one of those words that you don't just say—you smile and almost sing it. It just makes you feel good! In Italian, we say "ciao" for both hello and good-bye, just like they use "aloha" to mean both in Hawaii. *Aloha* means many things: hello, good-bye, peace, compassion. And when I see my good friends or my family, and we say "ciao" to one another, I feel that same thing. It's more than a greeting. It's a little burst of sunshine, a wish for happiness in their day.

Hawaii is one of my favorite places to visit, and I am so excited to share it with you!

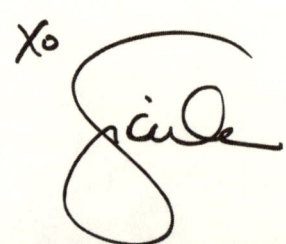

And now, a taste of
the next book in the series,
Recipe for Adventure:
Miami!

Chapter 2

"How about a lunch break?" Zia asked.

"Yes, please!" Alfie and Emilia said in unison. Alfie, as usual, was starving, and he knew Emilia was looking for any excuse to take a break from her routine.

"Great," Zia said.

Zia put her arm around Emilia and led her into the kitchen. Alfie followed close behind. Emilia was still quiet. "I know you'll figure it out," Zia told her. "Don't get so down on yourself."

Emilia nodded and managed a small smile.

Alfie took his usual place at the kitchen island and waited for Zia to assign him a task. Zia opened the refrigerator and pulled out honey mustard, butter, some deli meat, Swiss cheese, dill pickles, and arugula. "What are we making, Zia?" he asked.

Zia took some whole wheat rolls out of the bread box on the counter. "We are making *Cubano* sandwiches—with an Italian twist."

"*Cubano*?" Emilia asked. "As in Cuban?"

"That's right!" Zia answered.

"I've never had a Cuban sandwich before," Alfie said. "Let alone an *Italian* Cuban sandwich!"

Zia laughed. "Well, you're going to love my version."

Zia put the cutting board on the counter and sliced each of the long wheat rolls in half horizontally. Then she pulled a couple of dill pickles out of the jar and cut those into long thin slices as well. She slid the bread toward Emilia. "Spread some honey mustard on each half of the roll. Then Alfie, you add a slice of Swiss cheese to the bottom half."

"Okay," Emilia and Alfie said.

Once their ingredients were added, Zia piled several pieces of meat on each sandwich.

Alfie, Emilia, and Zia worked on their sandwich assembly line. Alfie's stomach growled loudly. "I like Cuban sandwiches already," Alfie said. Zia laughed.

"The first time I had a Cuban sandwich was . . . ," Zia started.

"In Cuba?" Emilia offered.

"Nope, in Miami. There's a very big Cuban population in Miami."

"When were you in Miami, Zia?" Emilia asked.

"I've been there several times," Zia replied. Zia hadn't only sent Alfie and Emilia on adventures all over the world, she had traveled a ton herself—exploring places from South America to China and everywhere in between.

"Wow!" Alfie said. "You must really like Miami."

Zia smiled. "I do! Miami is warm and sunny, and the beaches are beautiful. And since it's so close to the

Caribbean, there's a lot of great food and culture there."

"My social studies teacher told us that more people speak Spanish in Miami than English," Emilia said.

"She's right," Zia said. "I definitely learned some Spanish in Miami. Sometimes it feels like you're in a Latin American country because the influence of those cultures is so strong there. Miami is very proud of its multiethnic heritage."

"That's cool," Alfie said. "I bet it would be a lot more fun to learn Spanish in Miami than in Mrs. Vega's class."

"Being surrounded by a language every day is a pretty quick way to pick it up," Zia said.

Zia added the top to the last sandwich and pressed each one down. Then she put a pat of butter in the skillet along with a drizzle of olive oil. She turned on the heat and Alfie watched the butter and oil melt together and start to bubble.

"Hand me two of our sandwiches, Alfie," Zia said. "The pan's almost ready."